Abo

Derek Smith has lived most of his life in the East End of London. He has for many years been involved in community projects in the area: as writer-in-residence for Soapbox Theatre in Newham, as one of the founders of Page One bookshop in Stratford and as a co-op development worker in Tower Hamlets. He has had plays performed on radio, television and the stage. More recently, he has written nine books for children, including three novels published by Faber.

Strikers of Hanbury Street & Other East End Tales was first published in 2002 by Rhapsody.

Other books by Derek Smith:

The Prince's Shadow
Hell's Chimney
Catching Up (poetry)

Children's books:

Hard Cash
Frances Fairweather – Demon Striker!
Fast Food
Baker's Boy
The Good Wolf
Half A Bike

Books for younger children:

Jack's Bus
The Magical World of Lucy-Anne
Lucy-Anne's Changing Ways

Strikers of Hanbury Street
& other East End tales

Derek Smith

Earlham Books

First published by Rhapsody 2002
by Earlham Books 2010
New edition by Earlham Books 2013

The right of Derek Smith to be identified as author of this work has been asserted in accordance with Section 77 of the Copyright, Design and Patents Act 1988

ISBN: 978-1-909804-02-9

Contents

To Pat & Lew

who lived most of their lives in the East End

Introduction

THE first edition of *Strikers of Hanbury Street & other East End Tales* was published by Rhapsody in 2002. This second has, in addition to the tales, this new introduction and nine previously unpublished poems.

The stories were written over 25 years, the earliest dating from the mid-1980s. Two were broadcast on BBC Radio 4's Morning Short Story (*The Case of the Hackney Man* and *The Boatman*). Some are historical, some have become historical. The main character of *Quarter of a Millionaire*, for example, dreams of becoming exactly that. But house prices have shot up since the late 80s and, if still alive, he might be worth a million or more now. But the title, *Quarter of a Millionaire*, has the air of the ridiculous about it, while millionaires are not what they used to be.

I have spent most of my life in the East End. My first memories are of a damp basement flat in Hackney; the people upstairs had a fierce Alsatian which terrified me. *The End of Captain Marvel* is semi-autobiographical and is set in Hackney as we are preparing to move to Poplar, which we did just before the Coronation, on to LCC flats in Bromley by Bow: the setting for the story, *The Daughter's Visit*.

While brand new in the early 50s, the flats rapidly became slums. With renovation, they have improved since but remain bleak. Except they weren't to me when I lived there. What, after all, did I have to compare them with? At secondary school in biology, I remember having to copy the cross section of a primrose – a flower I had never seen. They didn't grow on the bombsites of Poplar. Or maybe they did, and I trampled them.

We moved back to Hackney in the 60s but I continued at my school, George Green, on the East India Dock Road, travelling there by the 106 bus through Bethnal Green. I recall a smattering of the school song:

St George for merry England shout,
A champion, staunch and true.
Our own good knight fought ignorance,
St George for Poplar too!

Deconstruct that, if you have the time. Perhaps telling you that the school was a grammar school might assist. And that George Green was a shipbuilder of 150 years ago. I leave you to connect him to a Palestinian of the 4th century and to make what you will of 'merry England'. Symbols and clichés have a strange hold on us.

In 1976 I moved to the London Borough of Newham to join Soapbox Theatre as a playwright, and remained in the borough when I left them, living at various times in West Ham, Plaistow and Forest Gate. The nine poems included here were written in 2011 when I set myself a project: to visit various sites in Newham, to take a photo and to write a poem about each place. I thought of adding the photos to this book, but, on investigating, found their presence would totally dominate the choice of page size and layout of the book to the detriment of the writing. So, as I say to a class of infants when I read them one of my children's stories, you must imagine your own pictures. A poet always hopes their words are strong enough for that.

After a reread, I am aware of what's omitted in these East End Tales. There are no Chinese characters, no Eastern Europeans or Somalis. My only excuse is that I have written about those I have encountered. And, perhaps, left myself room for a third edition in ten years.

Forest Gate, June 2013

My father, who was born in 1911, lived on Hanbury Street, off Brick Lane. He told me a story of how, as a boy, he and his friends picketed a man's house to get their ball back. Their inspiration was the London Jewish Bakers' Strike. It was his first political action; he went on to become a trade union activist. This story was written in 1988.

Strikers of Hanbury Street

L AST week I went to Izzy's funeral. I knew him when he didn't have a proper pair of shoes to his feet, and he ends up in the House of Lords. What a come down for an old Communist! We joined the Party together in 1931, but Izzy went soft and threw his lot in with the Labour Party instead. So there you are. But who should I meet at the funeral but another pal from the old days, Morry, who when he retired was a partner in a firm of West End accountants. The friends I've got! We had a chat, compared our respective lives. And ended up in an argument about trade unions. I'm embarrassed now to think about it; a couple of silly old men shouting at a funeral. One of Izzy's sons had to ask us to have respect.

So we quietened down and had a joke about it. Morry called me a born troublemaker. I told him not born, and I reminded him how I got into politics. My first action. It was us versus Mindel the sweater, and we were on a hiding to nothing. Let me tell you about it. But it's no good beginning in the middle; I'll start when we saw the London Jewish Bakers.

Me and Morry and Izzy were just kids, wandering up the Whitechapel Road. I had to pick up some leather for my dad and the others came along. I had the hides under my arm wrapped in brown paper. The road was bustling with lorries, buses, horses and carts. And the streets crowded with people going everywhere.

If you think Whitechapel is crowded now you should have seen it then. That's one the things I always

11

remember about my childhood. It was hard to be alone. People in the streets, people in the houses – there were six in our family; my mum and dad, my brothers and sisters. We only had three rooms, and one of those was Dad's workshop so it was always noisy. When all of us were there it was a problem finding a seat. And yet we were well off compared with some. Izzy's family – there were seven and they just lived in one room in Princelet Street. It was right at the top of the house and used to stink of piss and cooking. The whole house just had one outside toilet. But it was not only people in Izzy's place; his mum had her sewing machine which was always rattling away and there were piles of clothing she'd be working on, amongst everything else. It was a madhouse.

Izzy had a job which he used to do before school. He had a wheelbarrow and had to take papers from Yankel's, the Yiddish printers, to the newsagents. I've seen his barrow piled so high he could hardly move it. And they used to yell at him for being late. Well everyone did. The Yiddish printers, the newsagents, and then our teacher. And what was worse, out of all this he hardly saw a penny. His dad took it and gambled it. His mother used to keep the house, when she wasn't machining, and his dad took most of her money as well. I have seen Izzy, his feet coming out of his shoes, with snow on the ground. My dad saw him. He said, "Come in, Izzy." Then he repaired his shoes. He said, "Never walk round like that again. You come and see me."

Morry, though, was always well dressed, and his parents didn't like him playing with Izzy. Well, Izzy was a ragamuffin and Morry's dad was a tailor and religious. Whatever you say about religion – my dad being an anarchist we never had a lot of time for it in our house – but religious people kept their houses better. There was always food about. I never liked going to Morry's place because they would always ask me questions about was I going to *schul*, and was I going to *chaddah*, and what had we done over the fast – and I had to tell lies. But sometimes they would give me a bit of *chola*, even on a week day. One day I remember I even had chopped herring on it. His mother always seemed to be cooking, and the smells! I remember going once and she was frying fishballs. There was a plate of them on the table. Mouth-watering! Heaven must be like that – if there is such a place. I was waiting for Morry, and she kept asking me questions as she was rolling the balls in her plump hands and I couldn't keep my eyes off the plate. Beautiful brown balls. Oh!

Well, on this day we were watching the march. The London Jewish Bakers were on strike and they were marching down the Whitechapel Road towards Aldgate. There were hundreds of them, and they weren't wearing overalls and aprons, but just ordinary clothes. At the front they had a big banner saying who they were over a picture of men putting bread in an oven. Underneath it said "Buy Bread with the Union label."

I knew a bit about it because my dad told me. They worked all the hours, lots of night work – well you know, to get the bread out for the morning. Terrible conditions, bad pay – the usual. But it was skilled work. Jews like their bread. Cholas, rye bread, beigels, platzels, matzos, biscuits and cakes. Hooman taschen – that's what I liked; sticky pastry, full of sweet poppy seeds. Mmmm.

We gave them a cheer. How could you eat bread, said my dad, if you knew the man making it couldn't feed his family?

Nearly everyone on the road gave them a shout. We all knew how hard they worked.

While we were watching Izzy gave a yell and dived down to the gutter. He had found a penny, and danced around as if it were a gold sovereign. Then he went running off while me and Morry watched the last of the march. In a minute Izzy came back again with a bundle of broken biscuits wrapped in newspaper. He offered them to us. I took them. Morry was hesitating. They're not kosher – are they? In the end he gave up and ate them, looking around all the time in case someone should see. Well if Morry goes to Hell I'm sure it'll be for more than a few broken biscuits.

We cut through the back streets to Hanbury Street where I lived. My dad would be wondering about the leather.

I left the two of them outside while I went in the house. Dad had the front room of the house as his workshop. He was there in the dust, the sunlight spinning through on to his bench. Always that smell of leather dust. A shoe on a last and pins in his mouth. He could bang them in so fast you could hardly see his hand moving. On one side of him his row of knives, on the other his leather needles. Behind him on shelves, shoes that he had mended. At his feet a pile of shoes waiting to be done. And the floor a mess of leather strips and cut outs.

I gave him the leather and told him about the march. He stopped his hammering. "Did you give them a cheer?" Nails were sticking to his lower lip.

I said we did.

"Capitalism," he said as he hammered, "is good for bosses, landlords, and wars."

"It makes the rich richer and the poor poorer," I said.

"Correct."

My dad was small and dark as if he was stained with the leather he worked with. His hair was grey and wiry and his hands very thin. But the thing about my dad I always remember – he never got angry. He got sad and cried, like when they told him my sister Leah had tuberculosis – but he never shouted.

I was just going to leave when he called me.

"It's your birthday Tuesday."

I nodded.

He stuck a hand under the bench and came up with a football.

"Catch."

It was beautiful. Not full size, maybe three quarters – and I knew he'd made it. I recognised his stitching in the panels and the smell of the polish on it. It was reddish brown and blown up hard. I ran my hands round it, the soft animal feel of good leather.

"Smashing."

"It's not every day you're ten," he grinned showing his gold tooth.

"Hey Mum, look at this!" I ran into the kitchen. She was there with Golda, my older sister who had just lost her job in the clothing factory. Golda was mending a dress, my mum was pounding dough on the table.

My mother saw me with the ball in my hands. She dropped the dough and slapped a hand to her face. "Where did you get that?"

"Dad made it."

Quickly she was across the room and took the ball off me. Then into the workshop.

"What are you giving the boy? You think we live in Victoria Park?"

Between hammering, he said, "What's he ever had?"

"And what about me? Or your daughters? What have they ever had?"

My dad called. "Golda!"

Golda put down her dress and went out to the workshop.

"Do you want a football?" he said without looking at her.

"Like a hole in the head," she sniffed and went back into the kitchen, giving me a wink as she came in.

My mother came back. "*Mshuga*. A football – to break every window, to run under the horses. A football. Why don't you take up violin?"

My mother was small and round and always wore a full apron, looped over her head and tied round her waist. She had all the anger in our family. Her face was soft and puffy like a baked apple.

I took the ball and went out into the street.

Before I could show it, Izzy had it off me. I chased him and he threw it to Morry. So we played piggy in the middle. My mum was right of course; Hanbury Street is not a main road but busy enough. We dodged between the wheelbarrows and the horses and carts, risking life and limb.

But it was such a ball. None of us had played with a real football before. If we wanted a game we would make up a bundle of rags and kick that about – but a leather football. Who could believe it?

Each time I caught it I would feel it, like a pet animal. Mine, my beautiful ball. That is until Izzy threw it into the horse manure. I was going for it and he did it on purpose.

That made me really angry. My new ball all covered in dung! I would have punched him on the nose but Morry said let's kick it about a bit until it cleans off. Izzy said he hadn't meant it, but he had all right, he had chucked it right in with both hands. So I said OK – but only if Izzy goes in goal.

Izzy agreed. He could see how angry I was. He stood against Mindel's wall and we chalked two posts, and me and Morry kicked it at him. I think he was enjoying it. Getting the ball I mean. We would pound one at him then he'd pick it up in his hands like a real goalkeeper, bounce it along, or even clutch it to himself. What was a bit more dirt to Izzy? Then he'd throw it out and try to hit one of us.

He got Morry with a mucky bit of the ball. Morry sat on the kerb picking the bits of manure off, face screwed up. He kept smelling his coat, picking a bit more off, brushing himself down with a bit of paper and then smelling himself again.

"Lucky it's not pig, Morry," I shouted.

"It's all over me. My dad'll beat me."

Just to show how little he cared, Izzy headed the next one at him. It hit Morry on the back. Morry picked the ball up in a rage. He doesn't get angry often but when he does – get out of his way.

Morry put the ball on the spot. "Too close!" shouted Izzy, pressing his back to Mindel's wall. For an answer Morry rubbed it in horse dung and put it a yard closer.

Izzy stood there in terror as Morry came in to slam the ball at him. It was Judas Maccabeus versus a freshly clipped Samson.

He needn't have worried. There wasn't a chance of it hitting him with Morry as angry as that. It went high over his head, and Izzy, just to show that he wasn't really scared, dived for it. He touched it with his fingers and tipped it over the bar. If he had been at Wembley that would have been fine – but it was Hanbury Street. And the ball was in Mindel's yard.

We had a blazing row. Morry said it was Izzy's fault, he didn't have to dive for it. Izzy said it was Morry's fault and the ball was going over anyway. I said it was both their faults – and which of them was going to get it?

We knew Mindel, a sour man, his wife just as sour. He would walk the street with a brown paper bag collecting string and bent nails from the gutter. Aaron, their son, went to our school, always in clothes two sizes too big. He was always picking his nose and chewing the bogies. Candles, we called him.

Mindel had a cellar under his house where six women worked for him in a dark room with bars on the window. You would have to be badly off to work for Mindel.

None of us wanted to go for the ball. So we dipped:

One potato, two potato, three potato, four
Five potato, six potato, seven potato, more.

Izzy won. Or he lost – because he had to go. We had to push him right up to the door, and we backed away leaving him there. He kept looking over to us, hoping we'd changed our minds.

"Go on, knock, Izzy," I called.

At last Izzy went up to Mindel's door, and knocked. He waited. Nothing. Izzy started coming over.

"Knock again," I called.

He crept back, head hunched in his collar – and then suddenly knocked so hard we almost ran.

Mindel opened the door. He was wearing crumpled trousers and an open dressing gown. Under it he had on a striped collarless shirt. He had a cupel on, I don't know why, he wasn't religious. Maybe it was stuck to his head.

"Whadja want?" he barked. "I'm a busy man."

We could just hear Izzy.

"Our ball went into your yard, Mr Mindel."

He scratched his face. It was dirty with maybe three days' growth of beard.

"What's a *schnorra* like you doing with a ball?"

"It's not mine, Mr Mindel…" He pointed helplessly over to us.

"More *schnorras*." He began to close the door. "There's no balls in my yard." The door shut.

I was so angry I wanted to smash all his miserable windows. Or maybe that would have done him a favour and let the lice out. Morry said we should knock on his door hard and run away. Izzy said we should shovel horse dung through his letter box.

"I'll have to climb into his yard," I said.

Morry didn't think that was a good idea. I told him he didn't have to as it was me doing the climbing not him.

The wall was two feet over my head. I needed a heave up. Izzy got down and I stood on his shoulders against the wall. With Morry's help he slowly stood up and raised me up. The wall had glass on top, and so I doubled Izzy's jacket and threw it over. He said it couldn't make his jacket much worse.

I pulled myself onto the wall and sat astride. The yard was packed with junk reaching up to the top of the wall. Broken tea chests, rusty tins, scraps of broken fence wood, chicken wire, bundles of newspapers, useless bits of furniture, a big black pot with a hole in it. Everything that Mindel ever had – except my ball.

I climbed down onto the junk for a better look round. The back door opened and Mindel was there.

"I caught you, you thief."

He grabbed a fence post and prodded at me at the same time as I was making my way back. I caught his face, his lips were pursed, and he was digging at me as if I were a rat. If he could he would have pushed me off the wall. I took hold of the post and tried to hold it off me, so I could climb back over. It snapped.

Astride the wall with the broken post in my hand, I looked down at Mindel amidst his junk. I knew he couldn't climb up and get me; all he had on his feet were carpet slippers.

"I only want my ball, Mr Mindel."

He picked up a tin can and threw it. It missed. In the next instant I was back over the wall and down on the ground. It was only when I was down I realised I had left Izzy's jacket.

If it had been mine I would have left it and taken the consequences at home. But I couldn't leave Izzy's. It was all he had.

He hoisted me up again.

I was getting it off the glass spikes as Mindel's front door opened. Our human pyramid collapsed. Fortunately I had the jacket. I picked myself up and ran off with the others, with Mindel cursing after us.

We came into Brick Lane. He wasn't following. He would have died, I think, if he left his rubbish. It was then Morry came up with the idea. The last good idea he ever had.

"We should go on strike," he said.

Of course he'd got it wrong. We didn't work for Mindel so we couldn't strike. I told him he meant picket.

"And march," added Izzy.

Morry was already getting sorry he thought of it but me and Izzy were getting excited over the idea.

"Let's leave it," said Morry. "It'll just cause more trouble."

Me and Izzy started laughing and thinking of all the trouble. Izzy said there'd be police charges and the gang leaders would be arrested. I said more like they'd shoot us the same as they did in Sydney Street.

Morry sat there looking miserable. That's the problem with religion – it makes you miserable all the time.

"We need to make some banners," I said.

"I'll go up the carpenter's workshops in Hackney Road for sticks," said Izzy.

"Cardboard," I said. "I'll go up the shops."

"I'll get some tailor's chalk from my dad," Morry put in reluctantly.

None of the stuff was difficult to get and within an hour we were back with it. Izzy had somewhat overdone it.

"I thought I'd sell firewood when we finished."

We decided to hold one banner each. It wasn't difficult finding slogans to put on them:

Mindel – the ball stealer
Mindel – exploiter of the working class

That one didn't have much connection with our ball, but we all liked the word 'exploiter'. The trouble was I started off writing too big and had to squeeze working class in, so that it was very small near the bottom.

Mindel the schnorra wrote Izzy for the third. Morry didn't like that. He said it would just make him more angry and get us in more trouble. What he really meant was that it would get him in trouble. Izzy said he didn't have to hold it.

When we had written them, we made them up. I'd managed to sneak a hammer, small saw and nails out of Dad's workshop.

"Where we going to march from?" asked Izzy.

"From here. Up to Gardiner's Corner," I said. "All marches go there. Then back down Brick Lane."

"We can't march here," protested Morry.

We both looked at him. "Why not?" I said.

"We just can't."

"What's the point of making banners then?" said Izzy.

Morry was getting more and more upset. "The whole thing is just stupid."

"You mean it's too near your dad's?" I said.

"I mean you lost your ball, and marching to America wouldn't get it back." He had put his banner down and was leaning against the wall playing with the ends of his jacket. "I thought it was just a game."

"Come on, Morry. You thought of it," I said.

"Well a boy can change his mind – can't he?" he said angrily and started wandering off. "Why should I get a hiding?"

Watching him shamble off took the energy out of me and Izzy.

"Morree! Come on…" Izzy called after him, but Morry didn't even turn back. Izzy looked at me, I looked at Izzy. Should we, shouldn't we? In my time I've fought enough hopeless battles, but how can you just do nothing? Isn't the defeat worse then?

"Let's go," I said trying to sound enthusiastic.

"What about his banner?"

"Pick it up on the way back."

We got into the roadway, and walked side by side with our banners on our shoulders.

We turned into the bustle of Brick Lane. People, shops with their wares taking over half the pavement, a smell of pickles and straw, of horse manure and dust. In the road were men with carts, pushing them, pulling them. A few newish ones and a lot more that just seemed to be held together with spit. Horses and carts rattled by, and the occasional impatient lorry.

They shouted all around us. Horse whips cracked about our ears. Men with barrows cursed us as they pulled by. On the pavements passers-by stared at us. Some blankly, others hollered for us to get out the road. The two of us walked on trying to look only ahead, assured of the rightness of our cause, and feeling very misunderstood.

When I think of it now I suppose it was only natural. What does *Mindel the ball stealer* mean halfway down Brick Lane? And even the one I had, *Mindel exploiter of the working class*, didn't mean a lot if you didn't know Mindel.

We were near the top of Brick Lane and so far we hadn't got any public sympathy. Just abuse by road users and pedestrians. A lorry driver had driven right up close and made us nearly jump out of our skins by hooting his horn. As he came past he wound his window down; a burly man, with a bright red face, and he spat.

"Go back to Russia!"

We turned into the Whitechapel Road. I was wondering how to give up without being the one to say it. I didn't want to walk down Brick Lane again.

As we turned into the main road where the pavement widens, there was a crowd of men, all facing a man on a step-ladder who was shouting. He had a thick moustache, bushy hair coming out of a bowler hat and his arms were winding like windmills. Then for no reason we could see he stopped shouting. He took off his hat, grinned and pointed at us. The crowd turned about.

"Hold up your banners young 'uns," he shouted.

Somewhat surprised, we did.

"Mindel?" he shouted over the crowd. "Is that Mindel the master tailor on Hanbury Street?"

"Yes," I called. "He stole our ball."

"The dirty dog. My sister worked in his cellar for flunpence an hour. Come here, comrades."

The crowd opened like the Red Sea, a mass of faces staring at us. We came cautiously forward, holding our banners up. Moustaches, hats, open collars, and men's faces like bobbing apples. The path they had opened led down to the man on the step-ladder.

The man broke into a beaming smile and began to clap us. Then everyone was clapping and cheering.

When we came to him he bent down to us. I could smell *wurscht* on his breath. "Do you know who we are?"

"The London Jewish Bakers," I said, having seen one of the banners as we came through.

"And what do you think of us?"

I shouted, "You work too hard for the money you get."

That brought a cheer from those who heard me at the front. The man on the ladder repeated what "the young comrade" had said to the rest of the meeting. And everyone cheered.

"What are you going to do now?" he asked.

"March back to Mindel's," I said, "and picket him."

He repeated what I said to the crowd and they all laughed. That made me go all red and prickly. Why should they make fun of us?

"Comrades!" the man called out to the meeting. "These boys are the cutting edge of the class struggle. It is for them we fight."

The crowd cheered. At the back a few hats were thrown in the air. I smiled. I knew they were on our side against Mindel, and against men who spat from lorries.

While they were cheering the man bent down and whispered, "Get going."

Izzy and me turned about, and with our pickets raised began to march back through the crowd of workers. They opened again for us as we came. We went through them and turned into Brick Lane. I looked back. The speaker was a few yards behind, and the rest of the crowd were turning round and picking up their banners.

It was a very different march down Brick Lane from the two frightened kids who'd walked up it. There was Izzy and me with our two banners followed by the large banner of the London Jewish Bakers. And behind that all the smaller pickets held by the marching workers.

No carters shouting at us. No spitting lorry drivers. On the pavement people shouted for *us*.

Chanting began from the back. A man somewhere in the middle was shouting the Mindel lines and then everyone joined in with the response.

"Mindel the tailor!
Go to Australia
Mindel the sweater!
Don't write us a letter"

Ahead of us were people on the pavement, coming out of shops, wondering what all the noise was. From the other side of the road the passing barrow men and carters waved or showed a fist. I kept looking behind as if I needed to check they hadn't gone away, although I could hear the chanting. The speaker was at one end of the main banner. His bowler hat was thrown halfway back on his head and his curls blowing in the breeze. He gave me a big beaming smile and a thumbs up.

We turned into Hanbury Street with people following us along the pavements. The usual street crowd; kids, unemployed, beggars and *schnorras*. And the plain curious; we Jewish EastEnders are a nosy bunch – none of us know how to mind our own business. The gossip had run ahead of us like soapy water down a step.

As we passed our house Mum and Golda came out. Mum saw me and yelled into the house and, as we drew level, Dad came out. Mum was looking at me, and at the same time talking furiously to Golda. Golda gave me a wave and a big smile. She would. Golda was always on my side. Dad shouted something but it was lost in a chant that had just begun.

Me and Izzy stopped across the road from Mindel's. The army gathered up behind. We rested our banners, waiting for the marchers to come in. Mostly small men, in dark jackets, flat hats and homburgs – there was a lightness in everyone. In those men who had already been on strike for four weeks.

Me and Izzy were eyeing Mindel's house. We could see by the twitch of the curtains that they knew we were outside. The sound of our chanting would have penetrated the pyramid of Pharaoh.

The speaker came up to me. He said with his toothy grin, "Go and ask for your ball back now."

We started across the road followed by the bakers a few yards back. On the other pavements were the curious flotsam that had gathered in. Women in shawls pulled round them, men in cloth caps and threadbare suits, carters in overalls, their carts resting by the kerb, and the horses waiting patiently, striking at the kerb stones with their hooves.

We stood on the step, there were noises in the house, whispering and running about. We knocked. All the noise stopped. We looked back to the crowd. Dead silent, all watching us. We knocked again.

The door opened slowly, and a scared face came round. It was plump and careworn with thick grey hair like a horse's tail, and brown frightened eyes. It was Mindel's wife.

"What do you want?" she whispered, showing a mouth full of blackened teeth.

"We've come for our ball, Mrs Mindel."

She looked about her, agog at the crowd, tried to speak but words wouldn't come. The stout wall of bakers moved in tighter behind us.

"I'll get Mindel," she managed to say in a choked voice, and backed off closing the door.

Down below the house at that moment the cellar door opened and the women workers began to come out and to climb up the steps. They were bundled in their coats, tired pale faces wrapped in scarves.

The first woman up was a plumpish, short woman who waddled as she walked. "What's this – a wedding?" she called out.

She was close to me. "Mindel stole our ball," I said.

"I wish," she said with a grin, "you would steal Mindel."

25

The other women had come up and couldn't make up their mind whether to be amused or frightened by the crowd. The plump woman leaned down into the basement area and called in a sweet voice, "Mr Mindel, there's some boys want to see you."

She waddled up to me, big black buttons on her dark brown coat.

"What's your name?" she said.

"Jacob."

"Jacob," she said, "Mr Mindel is hiding under his cutting table. And for that…" She took me round the ears and kissed me smack on the cheek.

I blushed red.

"Give him one for me, Lil," called one of the women.

She smiled at me, and stroked my cheek. "I hope your mamma is proud of you. And all these men you brought."

The speaker of the bakers standing behind me called out, "Now why don't you join the union, ladies?"

She slapped her thighs and laughed, "Now that would give Mindel a heart attack."

She went over to the other women and whispered to them, and suddenly they were all laughing; rubbing their stomachs, tears streaming down their faces.

The front door opened, hardly noticed by anyone, and a small brown football rolled onto the pavement. I scooped it up, and ran around like I'd won the Olympic hundred metres. And the whole of Hanbury street set up such a cheer that I can hear it seventy years later. A cheer of joy, of unison. We were in it together. It was everyone's ball!

Me and Izzy were hoisted up shoulder high by the bakers and carried to Weavers' Fields, where they picked two teams and me and Izzy played goalkeeper in opposite goals.

That *was* a day. And the start of my political life. I learnt the people united could do anything.

All those years ago.

I hadn't thought about our picket for a long time, until I had my ding dong with Morry at Izzy's funeral. Then I brought it up to make the point I wasn't a born troublemaker.

"Aha!" says Morry, thinking he's so smart. "Suppose you hadn't met the London Jewish Bakers? And just the two of you marched back down Brick Lane alone, and stood outside Mindel's with your banners…"

Well, there was a thought. What if Hitler had got into art school, if Einstein had done botany instead of mathematics, if Columbus had got to India?

What if I were Morry and he were me? What would the tinker do?

But I knew the point Morry was making. What if I, renowned troublemaker, had lost my first political action. The archetype, the mould maker!

What if?

You've got to laugh. It was important for Morry, all those years later, to show me it was just self-interest. And why? Because Morry was defeated before he ever began. So he had to make the rest of us a monkey on a stick too.

I can't answer his question. No one can. But this I do know; ball or no ball, I wasn't destined to be a partner in a firm of West End accountants.

I love the Woolwich Ferry and am amazed it still exists. They keep promising a bridge over the Thames, east of Woolwich, which I hope never comes – as that certainly would kill off this free ferry service.

WOOLWICH FERRY

No Ernest Bevin today, just one at the quay,
a queue of traffic, container lorries, white vans;
the turn of James Newman, fat, panting dodgem.
Red arms and yellow vis beckon the lorries in,
fitting them on deck like a Chinese puzzle.
Foot passengers file down the walkway of the
  bridge,
out of the rain, into the bowels of the vessel,
maybe 12, but slatted seating for 300,
recalling the docks, Jack Dash days,
when the ferry would fill between shifts;
workers squeezing in, smoking Weights,
reading Mirrors and Daily Heralds,
off to the Royal Albert or the King George,
where avenues of cranes hauled goods from holds,
on bustling wharves, before the container raiders
pillaged the piers and swept upriver to Tilbury.

Lorries and cars aboard, a quick turnaround
for a slow crossing, beginning with a pirouette
and out to midstream on the poor man's yacht.
Throb of engine, shake of pistons, oily hum,
iron rivets, clue to a ringing birth in dry docks.
Brown, grey river, devoid of shipping,
the Thames Barrier poking out like trained seals
awaiting a feed of cubes from Tate & Lyle.

These the days of end time, no rapture,
as City Hall planners fly from London City,
to schemers in Edinburgh, Brussels, and Berlin,
without a glance down at the bug on the river.

If you wander the streets as early as six in the morning, you will see anxious mothers with pushchairs, or reluctant toddlers in hand, on their way to a childminder. Being at work all day, the mother can only hope the childminder treats her child well. This story was written in 1992. The price of childminders has gone up a lot since then.

Childminder

E LAINE ripped the blanket off. The little black girl did not move, lying exposed to the morning cold. Her mother sat her up and jerked her arms up and down.

"Sod you, taxi driver."

She could hear him snoring in the other room. What an hour to come back last night! When she had totally given up on him, in he came half-drunk with a bottle of rum.

Fine for him, party any time. Then sleep it off, drive round and let yourself in somewhere. She had no illusion that hers was his only key.

She massaged her daughter's face and held her body up straight. Sleep was flowing out of her and some dopey half-awakeness taking its place.

Elaine led her into the bathroom, and wiped the girl's stretchy-rubber face with the flannel. Her liquid brown eyes looked up at her mother.

"Want to go back to bed."

Said with that tough face that in daylight would make her mother laugh. Instead she took her daughter's hand, and firmly led her back to the bedroom where she rooted through drawers for clean clothes while May stood sullen like a house god.

"Take your pyjamas off!"

Sighing, her mother sprang to her and began. Daughter remained inactive, while mother in her impatience didn't feel at all gentle.

"Ow, that hurt me."

31

"Help me then. Arms up. Does it have to be like this every morning?"

May puzzled at the unfairness. All she wanted to do was sleep, not be washed and dressed and dragged.

Breakfast was silent except for the slurping of their spoons in the cornflakes. Elaine had the radio on quietly. A night-time disc jockey was speaking hushed intimacies. A record began with fierce drums; Elaine turned it down, fearing to wake Steve. He was dreadful in the mornings, the downside of his evening jollity.

She combed May's hair with an Afro-comb, she would plait it at the weekend. Coats on. She put her daughter's hood up, and tied round her a yellow scarf. In spite of the time, she was held by May's prettiness. Elaine bent and kissed her on the cheek.

"You're a good girl."

May leaned on her mother's leg.

A look in at Steve, the black boy lover – his blanket half off, showing most of his powerful arms and chest as if posing. A look of pain on his face.

His women taking revenge?

The lights were still lit on the outside balcony as they scurried down the stairwell. Her shoes rang on the steps, clacking into the morning darkness. Out in the courtyard, the shadowy blocks made walls to a sky that froze the last stars in splinters of cold.

Elaine struck out past the waste-ground pulling May along as if on a tow rope. The little girl half skipped, half pulled backwards, coming along in jerks beside her steadfast mother.

Oh those buses! Fifteen minutes late and she would lose an hour. That had happened twice last week. She could weep at the time she worked for nothing. If she could rely on the 7.05 – that would be fine – but half the time it didn't come, and her lost money rolled down the gutter by the bus stop.

For the last week she had caught the 6.45. It got her to the factory at 7.10, where she joined the gathering group of sleepy machinists standing outside the gate, waiting for Ramesh. When he came he always made the same joke – how women queued for him each morning. Directly the gate opened they rushed in, eager for warmth and to put their card through the clock, while Ramesh dashed round lighting the gas and switching on the lights. Within minutes every machine would be running.

May started snivelling. "Want to go home."

Elaine stopped, plonked her on a wall and dropped to her level.

"So does mummy, luvey. Mummy would love to go home. But no money if we go home. No food. Mummy's got to work."

"Don't want Mummy to work."

Elaine laughed, and caught a tear on her hand. "Walk with Mummy. You're too big to cry."

She slipped May off the wall, they walked on slowly.

"What noise does the cat make?"

"Meow, meow," responded the little girl feebly.

"What noise does the horse make?"

"Neigh, neigh," with a little more enthusiasm.

Elaine went through the barnyard, speeding up the walk as she felt May coming out of her mood. She mustn't miss her bus.

On the main road islands of humanity passed bleakly. The darkness had shut them down like shops. Blinds drawn, minds locked up. A woman in a very short skirt rushed past them with two children in a pushchair, the children lolling against each other like stuffed bonfire guys.

They turned into a red-bricked estate; the ancient blocks called Holly, Bracken, Elder, Sloe. As if the planners believed the magic of the words could turn the gravel green.

As they took the stairs May began to bawl. Her mother stopped, and sat on a step.

"That's enough," she said sharply, as the child attempted to tug her down the stairs.

"Want to go home." And threw herself onto the ground.

"I'm not having any more of this. Get up. May!" Forcefully she picked up the child under her armpits.

"Don't like."

Elaine was distraught. The light was coming, buses were going, and her bloody child who held her like leg irons was having a tantrum.

Elaine smacked her twice on the bottom, then dragged her up the stairs. The child was a dead weight, pulling back, sliding on her shoes.

When they reached the balcony Elaine picked her up, and slung her over her shoulder. She walked to the end and rang the bell, only then releasing May.

The door was opened by a middle-aged woman in curlers and plastic apron.

"She's playing up, Mrs Rogers," said Elaine. "I dare say she'll quieten down when I've gone."

"Gone?" said the woman, her face squeezing up, closing deep-set eyes, like narrow caves up a cliff. "I'm not having her."

"I beg your pardon," began Elaine, startled by what she hoped she had misunderstood.

"I don't want no more of your sort." She was already closing the door.

Elaine pushed against the door. "Mrs Rogers!"

Mrs Rogers was pushing back, and shrieking in vehemence. "I don't want her. I don't like her. I just did it for a favour. No more. It was a mistake."

"I'll lose my job!"

The door was pushing shut. "I can't help that. She's a little thief."

The door shut and Elaine went wild.

"What do you mean my daughter's a thief!"

Both fists pounding on the panes. For the insult, for the shock, for the bus timetable. It was as if she had walked into the wrong cinema, and was yelling for the projectionist to run the film she had paid for.

From inside, "Go away, go away! We don't want your sort."

Elaine opened up the letter box. There stood the little dried-up woman with a mop held like a bayonet. She prodded, and Elaine released the flap.

She looked down at May who was quietly whimpering in her hood, her dark eyes ringed with tears.

"We don't want this wicked woman."

*

Elaine noted down two phone numbers she found in the post office window. Her early bus had gone and she could forget the next too. If she could find someone just for today, then she could go in late and tell some story.

The first woman she contacted was annoyed at being woken, and said she already had too many, and the notice had been there months. She phoned the second with trepidation, waiting endlessly for the phone to be answered. A woman with a deep cockney voice answered. Yes, she could take her.

The day was saved! She hugged May, feeling sorry for her bad temper early on. She would only be an hour or so late. Elaine could talk her way out of that if she looked contrite enough. She strode through the streets, suffused with relief. She was still a working woman.

The block of flats was half boarded up with plywood slabs. Hardly any flats had proper curtains, mostly sheets or tablecloths. The rubbish from the chute spilled over the courtyard.

The door was opened by a stout woman, heavily made up, her green slacks too tight. She invited them in, making a fuss of May as she did so. May clutched at Elaine.

The sitting room smelt of rancid butter, the furnishings murky and brown as if they had all been stirred in the same stew pot. By the door was a broody cabinet, the top cluttered with True Confessions. An old large-screened television was on, and facing it against the wall was a sofa filled with five small children, each with their shoes off.

The woman talked non-stop; the nice dinner she would cook, and how they all went out to the park and played. Some of the children, she insisted, had been with her for years.

Elaine could not keep her eyes off the children who watched her in silence, mouths agape. But for their eyes, they might have been dolls glued into their places. Forcing herself she said, "I've some shopping to do." And began to lead May out.

"Don't you want to leave her here – get to know the others?"

"It's her birthday," exclaimed Elaine, desperation rising. "I want to buy a present. We'll be back in ten minutes. I promise."

Once in the street she picked up May and ran.

They crept off the rush hour streets into a cafe. Elaine had a tea, and May a fizzy drink. They shared a buttered bun. She had given up trying to get to work. It wasn't going to happen. There was May at her heels, and there she would stay. Elaine picked the currants out of the bun and fed them to her daughter.

"What did you steal?" she said.

May twisted her face and her body, and closed her eyes.

"Tell me," said Elaine, "I won't smack you."

In a quiet voice the girl said, "Biscuits."

Elaine said, "That's not stealing."

May sucked her thumb. Elaine went to pull it out of her mouth and stopped herself. Why did she have to leave her daughter? Pay people who called her daughter a thief if she took a biscuit, and had no respect for Elaine herself?

Because of the Gas Company.

When May was eighteen months old the gas had been cut off, and it was only Social Services managed to get it put on again. She had the debt hanging over her head for nearly two years. It didn't seem to get any smaller. In the cold of winter her gas fire was like a monster she was forced to feed. She would wake in the early hours, and go through the bills in rising panic to find out why, in spite of her payments, the figures still grew.

Then Social Security began to hassle her. She was cohabiting, they said. They seemed to think if a man stayed a few times he was keeping you. She felt spied on like a child, but dependent on them like a child. In the end she got a job to get away from them, and to end the tyranny of the Gas Company.

May was sucking noisily through the straw. It was so nice to be with her. Just to watch her like this. See her little serious face, and know she was safe. She bought another tea, more fizzy drink, and another cake for the two of them to share.

There were only a few others in the cafe, workmen having their first break of the day. Papers out, smell of eggs and grease. Elaine felt very young, like a truant. All it required was her granny to come into the shop and drag her out. She bent her head down on the table to May's level, and chucked her under the chin. May laughed and Elaine popped a currant in.

They stepped out into the sunny street, dappled with morning shadow. No granny. The stolen hours were theirs.

*

May was on the roundabout, legs stretched out, while Elaine ran her faster and faster, until she jumped on breathless, and the world whirled past in a gush of wind and spin. Elaine lay back, watching giant trees stretching like scaffolding to the twisting clouds, the sky rotating, as if there were a plug somewhere and the blue was rushing out.

She could see the spring in the trees, the tiny green leaves, and birds flying across the twisting sky and alighting in the mesh of branches, dabbed with greenness. She would have sewn twenty shirts by now.

"Up and down
To and fro
That's the way
The swing will go."

May had her head back and was kicking her legs into Elaine who stood in front of the swing. She loved to watch her face, the joy of May on the swings, even though she risked a kick in her own face.

"Hello."

Elaine turned to the greeting. A large blonde woman was putting her child into the swing. The child was dressed in a green, red and yellow outfit that Elaine had been making last summer. All that fussy stitching for the Peter Pan range.

The woman said, "I was watching you on the roundabout."

Elaine looked at her quizzically. She had a hushed loud voice, very BBC, that was both intimate and public – one of those who didn't care if the whole bus could hear. But she looked friendly, in a do-gooder sort of way. Her smile was freckly, her nose turned up and pointed. She was more powerful than fat. You could imagine her putting the shot.

"Push, Mummy, push," ordered May.

Elaine did as she was bid.

The woman began lazily pushing her own child. "Don't mind me – I'm having a crisis. I have them periodically." Her sigh lapsed into a weary smile.

Elaine had come behind May as she was swinging too high. The woman rested an arm on her shoulder.

"Don't you ever feel you are living a lie?" she said.

Elaine laughed. "Not when the sun is shining."

"I suppose I'm waiting for real life to start. Motherhood is supposed to fulfil you – isn't it?"

Elaine pursed her lips and didn't reply. Motherhood wasn't her problem; it was the rest of her life.

"When Jason was born I waited for it to come, that earth mother feeling. But I just saw him like a pet rabbit. Cuddly, dependent – but I could take it or leave it." She turned to Elaine and shook her head. "I feel very ungrateful – all those couples dying for kids."

"My mother didn't like kids," said Elaine.

"What did she do?"

"Dumped us on my granny who did."

The woman laughed and sank onto a swing, and began to push herself. The woman's child was slowing so Elaine gave him and May a shove. The woman pulled herself backwards and forwards, her face raised to the sky.

"I've a lover," she said suddenly. "And it doesn't work with a sprog."

"You need a childminder," Elaine said with a cackle.

The woman gave an outrageous laugh, and stopped her swing. For a second she could not speak, the laughter gripping her. She held up a hand to indicate a pause as she controlled herself.

At last she said, "Do you know one?"

"Me," said Elaine pushing May fiercely.

"How lucky," said the woman rising from her swing thoughtfully. "Are you registered?"

"Oh yes."

"Look I've got some shopping to take home. Would you come back to my place and talk it over?"

Elaine and the woman went to the woman's car, May holding her hand, and Jason in the pushchair; a grey plush affair, clean as new. The woman strapped Jason in the child's seat at the back of the car and apologised that there was no child's seat for May. In a swift movement she folded the pushchair and put it into an otherwise empty boot.

She drove easily and words burbled from her. It was as if she had no thoughts in her head, just the words she spoke.

"Last night I felt like the maid, privileged to sit at table. I cooked the flaming thing, and I'm there with my tongue hanging out while my husband and his cronies talk about their clients, and Jenny has us spellbound with the house in the Cévennes she is working on. What am I supposed to talk about – disposable nappies and discounts at Asda?"

Her kitchen was splashed in sunlight with long windows on three sides, and numerous shades of yellow on the walls, ceiling and units. One of the windows opened onto a balcony over a Docklands basin with new apartments opposite, and lock-gates that led into the river.

They kept half an eye on the children in the nursery via the monitor high in a corner. Their tinny voices pleasantly far away.

"I am so fed up, I can't take another day of it. Mary cleans the bloody place and I make tea for her. My husband thinks I should get pregnant again. I told him he should." She laughed a little wickedly. "My husband is a Tolstoyan man. Thinks women are only happy when barefoot with a bun in the oven."

In the monitor Jason was bawling and pointing at May on the rocking horse.

"If I don't sort my life out I risk losing my husband and my lover," said the woman as they made their way down the thick-carpeted stairs. "One I'll walk out on through sheer tedium, and the other will walk out on me – ditto."

May was taken off the rocking horse and put on the train. Jason then wanted to go back on the train. May went back on the rocking horse, and Jason on the train began to work up to another round of tears. At her mother's behest May got off the rocking horse. Jason then decided he wanted to play with neither, and began to jump up and down on a panda.

"Charles is an accountant. I'm his Docklands portfolio. I tell no lie."

Elaine thought of Steve. What did he call her amongst his friends?

"Very regular is Charles. You will find him at the office, in Horsham, or here. That being the case I only need a childminder one and a half days a week." Elaine's heart sank. "Actually three mornings. How much would you charge for that?"

Elaine said, "Seventy," and instantly regretted it as the woman simply nodded.

"I'd rather you did it here," she said wandering about picking up letters and jigsaw pieces. "Jason has all his toys here." She turned with a wry smile. "And the bedroom's upstairs. Do you mind? I'll pay your fares."

*

Out in the street beyond the wrought-iron railings Elaine wondered whether she was a childminder or not. It would be so easy not to turn up next Tuesday morning.

Seventy pounds a week was neither here nor there. It didn't solve her problems, but simply made them more complicated. It was not enough to live on, and yet it made it impossible for her to do anything else. Who wanted a worker that couldn't do Tuesday, Wednesday, and Friday mornings?

Maybe she could sub-contract? Maybe the woman had rich friends with lovers who needed a childminder for weekday afternoons?

May ran ahead of her down the porcelain sleeve that led under the river to Greenwich, her voice rustling like wind in tall grass. At work they would be eating their sandwiches over their machines. She and May would have theirs on the hill in the park, legs stretching over the river, feet in Docklands.

I went to George Green Grammar school in Poplar, near Chrisp
Street Market and the Isle of Dogs, at a time in the 1950s when
the docks were very busy. Since then the docks have moved upriver
to Tilbury and the Thames is empty, awaiting a function.

MEMORIES OF A RIVER

Skeletal cranes by busy wharves,
drawing crates out of deep holds,
banana boats from Jamaica, Barbados,
oranges from the Canaries,
corn beef from the Argentine, lamb springing
from New South Wales, working river;
the beating heart of trade and conflict,
battle ground of dockers and bosses.

Bridges shutting off the Isle of Dogs,
swing, cantilever, one bound to be working
against us, on the 56 bus route,
on the way to our games field
at the bottom of the island, docking
our football; work beating fun, always.

Tourist boats, loudspeakers: this wharf
that wharf when, there sugar, there calico,
the great fire, once when, brown green water
once the sewer, once the transport road,
quivering, splintering the sun, a view
for luxury flats – former wharves
and warehouses, a space for bridges,
still lithe, still strong, bending its way
through a steel & glass city, wider, wider
through Essex car and oil towns, to the estuary,
waiting.

East London has had many waves of immigration, usually following a crisis: the Huguenots, persecuted in 18th century France; the Jews after the pogroms in Eastern Europe in the late 19th century; the Bangladeshis in the 1970s after the war with Pakistan; and more recently Afghanis and those seeking to escape the ethnic conflict following the break up of Yugoslavia. The worst racists have often been poor whites, relapsing into tribalism when interacting with someone different. In this story, written in 1987, a racist and a black man discover common ground. I realised they would have to be trapped in some way or they wouldn't stay together.

The Boatman

"RIGHT," says Ted, "let's do him."

We are sitting on the wall, legs wide and stretched out across the pavement. We've all got crew cuts and Doc Martens. Mine are new, and polished red, like brick. They make you feel like you belong. They make you feel real.

Just then Bill comes. We always meet on the wall near the station. Sort of become tradition. Not that we got anywhere else. Now Bill's arrived it's a foregone conclusion. We're going for a bundle. Bill's little and likes to make out he's hard as anyone. He can be stupid with it. The last Man U game he'd have got murdered if we hadn't waded in.

"So what you say to him?" I says to Jean.

She looks at me cold, as if I had a cheek to speak, then says to Ted, "I says hurry up, you jungle bunny. Then he clipped me one."

"What we waiting for?" says Ted.

We follow Ted across the lights. He's all in denim with a six-inch gap between his boots and jeans. His sleeves are rolled up, even though it's cold, showing off his tattoo; a swastika with Mother written across.

You'd think we were a tank. People cross over. They walk round us into the road. They try so hard not to look at us – you know their eyes must be roasting in their sockets.

We turn into the park. I need to talk to Jean. I take her by the wrist and sort of hold her back while Bill and Ted kick a paint tin.

"Why do you keep touching me?" she says pulling away.

"I just want a word."

"Well you got one."

"What's wrong? I mean you bin ignoring me all morning…"

"You don't own me, you know."

I don't know what's up with her, and it's eating me up. Worse than you think. You see I've never had it with Jean. The fact is here I am sixteen, and haven't had it with no one. And now it's getting me; if I don't soon they'll think I'm queer.

Just then I catch a blow on my back like ten ton of bricks. I go flat onto the tarmac and catch me elbow a nasty bang. I know it's Bill. I've seen him doing it dozens of times. He charges up full belt into someone's back just to knock 'em down and see what they do. It's his way of showing he's harder than you. I can't back down on this one. Not with Jean here.

"Wanna hand up?" he says grinning.

It's such a boring trick, I know what he's about to do. I hold out my hand. As he goes for it, I go for his foot and pull him down. I cling to his boot and pull. Now he's writhing and kicking. His boot comes off in me hands. I chuck it into the bushes.

"I'll have you for that," he snarls as he hops off for his boot. No way am I going to get away with that.

"He's the one," says Jean. "That sambo." She's pointing out the boatman.

"Right, let's get a boat out," says Ted.

"Let's do him now," whines Bill.

"You don't know nothin'," says Ted, rubbing his hands, a quiet smile on his face. "How about we try something different? We get a boat out see? Then we row over to the

44

island. We're not supposed to be on the island – are we? So he has to come and get us…"

"That's nothing short of clever," says Bill.

The boatman looks about 50. He's not in any of that rasta stuff like the kids. Just a donkey jacket and flat hat. His face is thin and bony. He don't smile or look at us once. Maybe he knows something's up.

We pay up, leave the deposit, all friendly – then get in the boat. That's where the fun begins. Jean's on the rudder, Ted and Bill on the oars. I sit in the front and get wet. Soon as we're ten yards off we have a go.

"Jungle bunny, jungle bunny," Jean chants. "Get back to the trees!"

Ted yells how Hitler was too soft.

The man looks at us, his face twisted. He don't move for a second, then spits into the dust and turns away.

I'm watching Jean close. I'd been eyeing her up for three months before I got the bottle to talk to her. You know how it is, you don't want to act too keen, but you don't want to be too cool… so I did nothing and hoped to rescue her from drowning one day.

She asked me out in the end. I was blown over. Now when I think of it – I think she just needed a fella. Sort of to keep the flies off. I mean girls need fellas, cus all her mates had fellas, and I would do until someone better came along.

"Let's have the oars," says Jean and begins to move down the boat.

"Sit down, you old slag," shouts Bill.

"Who you calling an old slag?" she screams, and whops him round the face. Crack! The whole boat's rocking… Bill picks up the oar and goes to clobber her with it. Ted picks him up under the shoulders and, before he knows what's on, drops him in the drink.

Bill collapses in the water, then stumbles up sopping, covered in slimy weed. We roll up. The three of us are going on about the Loch Ness Monster. It's only luck we stop the boat turning over. Bill tries to get back in. Jean and Ted with an oar each keep pushing him away like a dog off a bone. Finally Bill gives up.

He wades away, out to the island, splashing like hell. He sits on the bank, emptying his boots, and giving us the two fingers.

We row over. Well Jean and Ted do. I jump out and pull us to the bank.

"Don't call me an old slag," says Jean. Bill keeps quiet.

"We'll light a fire," says Ted looking across the lake. "And wait."

The fire doesn't burn too well, all smoke, dead underneath with all the green wood Bill kept piling on. I slip my boots off, they're wet from all the splashing, and lay back under the smoke as Ted tells us about Feltham nick. How hard they were there. There was this guy they called the King, chopped someone's finger off for refusing him a fag.

"I thought I was hard but some o' them…" he whistles. "This bloke I met there, lives over Lambeth way – gonna get me a shooter. Then we're going to do a Paki post office."

I see Bill, standing up swinging my boots round his head by the laces. I go for him and he throws them up a tree. I push him against the trunk and bang his head.

"Me new bloody boots!"

He pulls away as I go to punch him. I leave him and begin to climb the tree. It's not an easy climb. I grab a branch over my head, and then walk my way up the trunk, still in bare feet. I'm gonna hammer Bill when I get down. I pull myself up and get into the crutch of the tree. Then work my way out on a limb. As I'm inching forward to the end where my boots are, I see the boatman arrive.

I look around for the others. Ted and Jean are in our boat, rowing off, and Bill is jumping in the boatman's and pushing it off. Now it's obvious what all the whispering was about when we were collecting wood. They're laughing fit to burst. Ted's got his arm around Jean. It's all too plain.

But I have to get my boots. Once I got them I can think what to do. They're still maybe three foot away, at the end of the branch.

"Stay where you are."

The man's staring up at me, cap back. He's very black, the skin tight on his cheeks, shiny. I stretch out again, then look to him. He's bouncing a stone in his hand.

"I need me boots," I say.

He shakes his head.

I reach for my boots. I'll have to risk his stone. My fingers tip the lace. I shuffle in – and feel a scratch on my sole. I jerk my feet away. He's prodding up with a branch about the size of an oar. He moves the branch sideways. Oh gord it's under me shoelaces…

Slowly he lifts the boots from the tree, holding them high and dangling, like two living feet cut off. He lowers them down to his hands. They hang from his fist which he holds up like a trophy.

I holler, "You do anything with those boots!"

In reply, he swings them round his head like a slingshot, and lets fly. Oh Christ – twisting and tumbling they arc over the lake, kicking at each other. And drop upside down into the water. One turns over like a cork, fills and sinks. The other tips, like a ship about to go down. For a second it stays – then slips into the water, leaving only a circle of ripples.

I look back to him.

"Bastard!"

Is it possible to hate him more?

He takes up the branch and without warning smashes it into the tree. The shock runs through me. The whole tree seems to shift. Then again. Thwack! My stomach jumps and is caught as it falls in the next thwack. On and on he hammers.

I clutch my branch and dig my toes deep into the crotch like a monkey hugging its mum. The blood swims in my eyes, full red at each bash, then smashing into splinters. I am terrified I will be shaken off.

Silence. I open my eyes, he is lying on his back on the ground with his mouth wide, breathing heavily. His donkey jacket is unbuttoned, flapping.

"You gonna let me down?" I yell.

"I'm going to eat you."

"What?"

"Eat." He demonstrates eating, putting imaginary food in his mouth and then sighing and rubbing his stomach.

"You know my race," he says. "You know what we do."

"You're crackers."

"Last week I lived in the jungle. Eating missionaries, or sometimes for a change, a nun. But now we are Christians – I sing a hymn first."

He gets up and pulls his jacket round him, and begins rekindling the fire. The sun is low and I am wet from the damp of the tree. A flame catches the wood.

"A black man can only light a fire," he says as he puts a twig into the flame, "but you, a white man, can light an atom bomb. I think if you wanted, you could launch yourself out of that tree and fly to the moon."

The fire crackles and the flames leap higher, the smoke twisting in the wind. He takes from his pocket a knife and begins to hone it on a stone.

"Let me down, mister."

"In a sandwich," he says, feeling the edge of the blade, before continuing his sharpening. "Why they left you?"

"They've gone. To get others."

He laughs, throwing his head back. "In a minute we'll hear the bugle sound and the cavalry galloping across the lake."

"Let me down, mister."

"I'm not stopping you."

"You said you'd eat me."

"When you're down. Yes."

What can I do? If I jump the ten foot he'll be on me. If I climb down he'll be waiting.

"Let's do a deal."

"You a friend of the Prime Minister? You can get me a Council flat?"

"You can't stay all night?"

"Can you?"

No. I ache everywhere. Where I twist I ache. I change position and ache. My foot's developing cramp. I bite my lip and stifle the pain.

"Tell me what you want?"

He shakes his head and laughs deep in his chest. "I want your soul, sonny boy. You see my black face – yessir it's the devil. And I want your soul. Then when I got it I want to turn it inside out. I want to look at the hate in the middle, dried like blood on a butcher's apron. And with this knife I'll scrape it off. Get under the hard bits, and shave them off the cloth of your soul. Then I'll put the hate into my little tin, and shrink you with my juju, to wear round my neck."

"Let me down, mister." All ache, no pride now. "Please let me down."

He has turned to the lake, red clouds above and below. "Can you sing?"

"No."

"Sing with me."

I don't know what I am singing. I sing the lines after him. The words are foreign and his voice goes up and down. I sing the pain in my feet. I sing my lost boots. I sing Jean and Ted. I sing my fear of this black man with his knife and his strange music.

He stops.

"That's a song from Nigeria. An old man is singing that his sons are too busy quarrelling to plant this year's corn. He tells them to sow the seed before they divide his land, and then divide the corn. He tells them divided land will not grow more corn."

Picking up his knife from where he had stuck it into the ground, he puts it into his belt.

"Come down."

I ease myself down the tree. There's a dodgy bit at the end, where I have my back to him. My knees are shaking so much I press them into the tree, dying for a pee. A sound behind me makes it flood out, down my leg. I wait until it stops – and jump the last five feet into a pile of leaves.

He is crouched by the fire looking into the flames. "I hate the way you make me hate."

"How do we get off?" I say, scratching and shifting in my collar.

"We wade."

We slip down the bank into the cold water, which creeps up our legs as we wade further. The weed on the bottom is slimy and my feet slip as I push to keep up. We swing our arms, and stretch our legs as if in slow motion.

He pulls a little way ahead and slows for me. The chill eats up my body. I stop for a breather, he stops. No sound other than our breathing.

He begins again, I come with him, stride for stride, breath for breath. The water is up to our waist, cold and dark green. It slips behind us. The bottom is soft, muddy and slimy under my bare feet. I cannot see the others anywhere but hear the black man's breath beside me. I can see our reflections, rippling and shadowy. Hard to tell which is which as we stride into them and break them up.

We come out of the lake and hang by the water's edge unwinding. I want to say something. It is aching in me to be said.

"Sorry." And I flush hot like a beetroot.

He sighs, throws back his head and looks into the sky.

"Me too."

The Greenway is grassed-over sewage pipes, about three miles long, running from north-west Newham, near the Bow flyover, down to the sewage works of Beckton. It is a popular cycle- and walkway, though it can be smelly in places.

SEWERBANK

Gurgling across the Lea, four pipes,
large enough to crawl through, flush out
North East London, faeces and toilet paper,
urine and tampons, the mush of a million closets,
a slurry of washing-up water, laundry lather,
bathing foam, a brown, lumpy soup on its way
to be digested by friendly bacteria, creators
of civilisation, the city's toilet attendants.

Combating Victorian shock, the injustice,
that all, every man jack, gets the pox
if chamber pots are tipped into rivers.
Cholera and typhoid do not stick to the slums,
but servant by servant, hand by hand,
carried by Marys to kitchen and nursery,
killing the lie of difference in the necropolis.

Grassed over, re-branded Greenway, a cycle,
a walk way, through small terraced houses,
cemeteries, parks, across streets, glugging,
like a monstrous gut, the city heaving,
as if after a year of constipation, out it pours,
a slurp and slap, hitting the lavatory of Beckton.
A long sigh, the gasp of release,
the thank god of discharge,
but wait, oh heavens, not again, quick, quick;
the creature cannot stay clean for five minutes.

I had a friend who learnt to pick locks from a book he got from the library. He then devised a system for clever robberies. I had another friend who was on the periphery of a large East End criminal family. If you were family or friend, they loved you. But if you crossed them – then leave town quick. How does it feel to be a mum to people like this? It is 1989 and Mrs Robert has no choice.

The System

BILLY finished wiping the egg, stretched and stood up. "I'd best be off, Mum."

"Sit down," I said.

He was halfway across the room straightening his tie. "What for? I'll be late."

"Late for what?"

That stopped him; he turned to me, startled. The quick shift of his eyes reminded me of his dad. Then he slunk his hands in his pocket and dropped into a chair.

"What?" he said, but he knew I knew. He'd be useless under questioning – his whole body gave him away. The only thing that shut up was his mouth.

"Let's have another cuppa," I said, "and you tell me straight."

I poured out, and just watched him, waiting for him to boil over like an overfilled pan.

At last he said, "Ask me."

"Why didn't you tell me you left your job?"

A long sigh, he spun away. "I knew it'd be like this." Then he turned to me with a pained look on his face that near broke me up. "The two of you expect the wrong things of me, Mum. I'm not like that."

"Like what?"

"Working for a living is like being in prison."

What happened next, so help me I didn't mean it, but I stretched out across the table and slapped him round the face. The smack of it silenced the room and his face flushed like a plum.

It was his dad's words. When his dad worked at Ford's for a few weeks, though you'd think it was ten years, he'd tell anyone who'd listen – how he'd be better off inside. Maybe it was just words – making him feel better for the number of times he was really inside – but sometimes I think he meant it.

The clink was his club. He knew the screws, he knew the cons. And he could forget all responsibility for us.

Billy was wiping his stinging face. A good-looking face, a bit thin maybe but with his dad's rich brown hair. I only hope he keeps it longer.

"You didn't have to do that, Mum."

"Tell me where you're getting the money to go on holidays to Egypt, buy a car, and new clothes."

"I won it," he said.

"Where?"

"On the Dogs."

I stared at him. Dog racing? I never knew anyone win on that, except the bookies. My mum used to say to my dad when he used to go over Harringay, "Greyhounds are less predictable than a baby's bum."

"How much did you win?"

He was wriggling in his shirt and gave me a look as if to see what was worth a try. A tight smile escaped.

"A lot."

"How much is that? Fifteen bob? Five hundred?"

He began to giggle, even though his face must have still been painful. He had to hold his mouth to stop himself, then signalled me to wait a bit. He gulped in a large breath and sucked in most of the laughter.

Through a face just holding together he said, "Twelve thousand."

"Lord God Jesus. You having me on?"

He drew out a bank book from his inside pocket. From it he took a bank statement and passed it over. There were a lot of figures on it, and I'm not too comfortable with figures. I looked back to him.

"Deposit column," he said. "Add it up."

There were only three numbers, big ones – and they added up to around twelve thousand.

"How can you win this much on the Dogs?"

He gave me a weak smile. "I got a system."

"Dogs don't run to a system."

"They do," he said. "And I got it."

I looked back at the bank statement. Money had gone in and money had come out all right. Quite a lot had gone out.

"How do I know that's Dogs' money?"

He gave me a big grin then, his front teeth were a bit crooked from the fight he'd had when he was a nipper; they'd mostly straightened up and I used to say they were the difference between him and Paul Newman.

"I'll show ya."

He rose and took my coat off the hook and held it out for me.

In the car I asked a few times where he was going. He just answered the same, "I'm going to show ya, Mum."

Billy's my youngest. Lord, I says, let me have one kid that stays out. Ivy and Lil are in Holloway. I used to be so proud of 'em, both married, living down in Canvey and Billericay. Their houses so smart, their kids dressed like royalty.

A mail order job they did, the two of 'em together. You know those catalogues? They had over 600 women in it, and getting £50 for each new member. They found them with 20 bank books under twenty different names. Trouble was they weren't brainy enough – they couldn't think it through.

Billy though, he's brainy – and if you're brainy, why not get a proper job instead of slopping out as a guest of Her Majesty?

And mostly he's been fine. Oh the usual shoplifting and whipping off the back of lorries, but nothing that mattered. He had GCSEs and got a job in a Council office when he left school. They let him go off on day release, and I was so proud to see him go off in the morning in his suit. Smart. I would watch from the window as he walked down the road, until he turned down by the hospital.

He was making progress.

Then came the day when I had to visit his dad and I went off, but when I got to the station I found I forgot my money, so I came back. And I find Billy there with half a dozen mates, and some girls – well I don't know whose daughters they were, but if I caught mine dressing like that… Playing cards, drinking beer – and a good job I come straight back n'all.

"Day off," he told me.

So why did I see him setting off for work as usual in his suit and briefcase? He forgot, he said. I kicked his friends out and phoned up his office. He'd left three months before.

And now he's trying to tell me it's all Dogs money? This car, it looks brand new.

"If you're into something like crooked credit cards," I say, "how long do you think that will last?"

He pulled into the kerbside, then turned to me. "I'm telling you, Mum – I got a system." He squeezed his cheeks and looked at me hard, then without turning away he opened the glove compartment, and put his hand inside.

"I'm just going into that betting office."

He withdrew his hand from the glove compartment. There was a gun on his open palm.

"Billy!" I howled, covering my face in my hands.

Then he was tugging at my hands as I pressed them harder into my cheeks.

"S'a joke Mum," he said soothingly. "S'a Woolworth's toy gun."

Slowly I withdrew my hands. He was looking at me keenly, concerned.

"Some joke." I was still crying.

"Sorry."

"It's not funny." Half a laugh escaped. Relief, I suppose. He put his arm round my shoulder, and I put mine round his. We stayed that way for half a minute as my tears slipped away.

Then he said, "Won't be a tick. You'll be all right?"

I nodded. He kissed me, and got out the car. Then stopped and grinned at me sheepishly.

"You'd better have this."

Through the open door he handed me the plastic gun. It didn't even look real now. Pity, I thought as he bounded across the pavement into the betting office. Who might I shoot?

I've been too obliging. Always there every visiting day. Dan at Parkhurst, the two girls at Holloway, Johnny when he was at Maidstone. Writing letters to 'em all, making out I was fine and coping. It's hard keeping that face up when sometimes all you want to do is cry.

It's why Billy's Council job meant so much to me. I wasn't born a Robert. My family are all hard workers. Dockers and builders. They earned their money.

I want one of 'em I can be proud of. I don't know what Johnny does and I don't want to ask anymore. The girls let me down, so that leaves Billy. Course he's my favourite. Well he's the youngest, and he always was a pretty one. I like having him at home. I wouldn't be able to cook for just myself. I need to feel needed.

Billy came out of the betting office grinning and threw a bundle of notes into my lap.

"What'jer think of my system?"

All afternoon I wondered what I thought. The money was real enough, and Billy left it with me. He didn't need it, he said. Over eleven hundred pounds.

I bundled it up and put it in the kitchen cabinet behind the cornflakes. I was still musing on it when Johnny came over. He's my eldest, he lives out in Hainault now but was over to organise Alice and Mac's do at the Grapes in the evening. It being their 40th anniversary.

He's always smart is Johnny. Too smart, and getting fat now, his face filling out as he loses his hair. I don't like his moustache. Makes him seem like some gypsy lothario.

We lost control of Johnny when he was a teenager. He went from bad to worse, and then when we thought he'd straightened out we found he'd got a lot worse. I remember meeting him up Stratford one day to buy a present for Lil's wedding and we popped into the Swan for a quick one. The whole pub went quiet when he came in and stayed that way the whole time he was there. Everyone gave us lots of room. There was a circle round us, like a glass ball. And then he had to go off for ten minutes to make a phone call, and the glass ball stayed round me.

It came back to me where I knew that before. Years ago when we hadn't been married long Dan knew the Krays and the Richardsons. Not that well but one of his cousins was an in-law of the twins, so he was sort of family. They were villains, oh nice if they liked you – but your life wasn't worth a scratch if they didn't. I remember being in a pub when they came in, and there it was – that glass ball.

I know Johnny is up to tricks. I never quite know what because no one will tell me. I've tried to get him to behave, but he just puts his arm round me and says, "It's all under control, Mum." What is?

We had a cup of tea and I asked about the family. Johnny asked me about Dad and the girls. I filled him in on what they said at visiting time, and showed Lil's last letter. While he was reading it, I suddenly burst out crying.

He stopped reading and asked me what's the matter. I didn't mean to tell him, but now he knew something was up, I told him I was worried about Billy, and all the money he was making.

At first Johnny laughed. I told him about the system.

"System!" he exclaimed. "The only system at the Dogs makes burgers."

He assured me he would have a word with him at the do tonight. I don't know that that made me feel any better. Johnny would either muscle him out or go partners.

I calmed myself down, tears weren't going to get me anywhere. And Johnny – now he saw I was all right – left me to get on with his arrangements. He would pick me up and take me over about 8-ish.

I didn't really need a lift, it's only a few hundred yards up the road, but I don't feel a woman should go to a pub on her own. A bit later Daphne came over to do my hair. She's a black girl, always spot on time, natters a bit but she does a good job, and reasonable with it. I don't like going to the hairdressers. All those silly girls chattering away about nothing and the men in there – well they're all a bit funny. I hate looking in the mirror wondering when they're going to stop.

She washed it, curled it, and darkened it here and there. It was a nice effect. Without hiding the grey and making out I was twenty years younger, she used it for a sort of tortoiseshell effect.

Billy phoned and said he wouldn't be in for tea but he'd see me at the do. I made myself some scrambled egg, had a bath, got dressed, and watched some telly until Johnny came.

The pub was full.

We had the saloon bar. Nick the Greek was at the door, a big man in a smart grey suit, with shoulders you'd think were padded but weren't. If anyone came that wasn't family or friends he put them right. He was polite about it, with a great big apology of a smile – but no one who didn't ought to got past him.

Jimmy Riddle was at the piano. I'm sure you know what that's rhyming slang for. I never knew his proper name. They used to call him that because he was always pissed – excuse my language – at the end of the evening. It didn't stop him playing though, nodding away like Hogey Carmichael waiting for Ingrid Bergman. He knew all the old songs. Music Hall, Bing Crosby, things like Showboat and

Chou Chin Chow – he went back a long way. But he never knew anything after 1960. He used to say Rock and Roll was all the same.

I sat down at the table with Alice and Mac and their family. I went to school with Alice. We were evacuated together in 1943 as schoolgirls, some horrible little village in Lincoln where they treated us like servants. The two of us ran away in the end, and hitched a ride off some soldiers down the Great North Road back to London. I never told Alice but Mac had asked me to marry him first, and when I said no because I was already keen on Dan – he asked her. I've often thought about the difference it would have made if I hadn't turned her Mac down. He's quiet, not like Dan except when he's had a few, a bricklayer. They got a council flat, and they've done it up very nice. She's certainly seen a lot more of Mac than I have of Dan these last 40 years.

But you can't change things – can you? You get what you've got and there you are.

Alice gives my arm a squeeze, and I give her and Mac a kiss and give them my present. It's a clock. When I can't think of what to buy, I buy a clock. People don't often buy clocks, I don't know why, and even if they do you can easily put another one somewhere – but who wants two chip fryers?

Johnny was paying for it all, Alice and Mac being like uncle and aunt to our kids, especially when we all lived on Star Lane. The bar staff were on yet there was no money involved – but to see all those tables with their glasses and bottles – I wouldn't like to work out the cost.

Johnny was at the mike doing his speciality; "Delilah". About 15 years ago he won a talent competition at Butlins, and I think he could've taken it up professional, like Tom Jones or someone. He's got a deep mellow voice, and when he sings "Delilah" he puts so much feeling into it that it's strange watching him – because he's never shown his emotions much, always been tight-lipped. I've not seen him cry since he was about nine. But there he was now crying out to all of us: "Oh my my De-li-lah".

Then Jimmy struck us up into a general sing song. *Mademoiselle from Armentierres, Any Old Iron, When Father Painted the Parlour, Goodbye Dolly I Must Leave You.* Then Ma Garrett, and she's eighty five if she's a day now, sang us a couple of the real old ones and we joined in the choruses. *Two Lovely Black Eyes* and *If It Wasn't For The Houses In Between.*

That last one I always try to work out where the man lives. You know – "With a ladder and some glasses, you can see to Hackney Marshes, if it wasn't for the houses in between." Except she always sings it too quick and by the time she's gone on about Chingford here and Wimbledon there I don't know where I am.

I'd had about five or six snowballs when I realised Billy wasn't there. I felt annoyed at him, all the worry he's giving me, and now late to Alice and Mac's do. Them of all people.

Johnny was introducing Mac to sing a song. A bit of a surprise for Mac but his face was all red and smiley so I knew the drink had brought him out. He gave a wink to Jimmy who started to play *My Old Dutch*. And Mac started to sing it to Alice. He hasn't got much of a voice but you knew he meant it. It was almost like there wasn't anyone else in the room.

We been together now for forty years
And it don't seem a day to much
There ain't a lady in all the world
That I'd swap for my dear old Dutch

Then Johnny came out from behind the bar with a huge basket billowing over with gladioli, dahlias, chrysanthemums – and Alice came up and kissed Mac, and that brought down the roof. Johnny took up the microphone and announced through the uproar that he'd arranged two weeks second honeymoon in Marbella.

Then Alice had a quiet word in Jimmy's ear. He gives a little nod and starts playing *If You Were The Only Boy In The World*, and Alice starts singing. Mac is looking pleased as Punch, and it's his turn to wipe back the tears. And I'm thinking they've been happy, they've got two good boys, and the girls – never had much money, but all the love they've got. And there's my Dan banged up, banged up twenty of the last forty years. And when our anniversary comes up in November he'll still be banged up.

Maybe it's the drink brings things out, but suddenly I felt so jealous. The nights I was at home with just a television set. I had a bit of a weep, and everyone thought it was for Alice and Mac.

Champagne it was then, and Johnny the jolly host ran round with trayfuls as fast as the bar staff could fill them up. We toasted the happy couple. We toasted them another forty years. And then Mac, looking straight at me, toasted "dear and absent friends."

Then that was all over, thank goodness, and everyone came back and we just drank and chatted. The laughter and voices in the room going up and down like the sea, and under it Jimmy Riddle playing tunes from Oklahoma.

Someone started talking about Star Lane, about how much better it was there. Maybe we had outside toilets and damp walls but we were together. We made it sound like the Garden of Eden. A bit of drink and you forget the National Assistance and Pa Garrett beating up Ma Garrett every time he came home drunk. And sleeping three to a bed, and Mum putting a mackintosh over us when it rained. Funny, the world through a drink glass – all one way or the other.

Johnny was getting really drunk. He was up by the piano, staggering, shirt open, singing *I Did It My Way*, I couldn't tell whether with agony or pride – but half the bar was as drunk as he was, so no one cared.

Then Joe, that's Lil's husband, signalled to me he was leaving as he had to get back to Canvey to pick up the kids, and I'd asked him to drop me home.

When I got back, there was Billy with his feet up in front of the telly.

I was speechless with fury. Here he was less than a quarter of a mile away watching Ginger Rogers in a film that wasn't much good 50 years ago. I turned it off.

He sighed and pulled himself up the armchair. "I meant to come, but you know – I got involved."

"Involved!" I blew up at him. "You selfish pig. How many 40th wedding anniversaries are Alice and Mac going to have?"

"I wanted to go. It just worked out I couldn't."

He was going to go on but caught my eye and shut up. I sat on the arm of the chair in fuming silence.

He got up, uncurling like a daddy long legs. "I'll pop along now then."

"It's good as over. Only the drunks are left. How long you bin here?"

He shrugged. "A little while."

"Don't you think about anyone except yourself?" My anger was fading. Disappointment taking over. You have dreams for your children. Maybe that's what our love is made of. And they break them like peanut shells.

He was holding onto a wooden chair, sucking his lower lip. "Couldn't be helped. My system. I had to go to the Dogs. Didn't mean to be that long."

"I'm going to get to the bottom of your bloody system."

He threw his arms up as if in pain. "I'm the only legit one in the family – and I take all the stick."

"Don't give me that!" I screamed throwing a cup on the floor. It didn't break but the tea in it spilled onto the carpet. I watched it soak in as if it were in a film. Then I dropped to my knees and began to mop it up with a handkerchief. It was next to useless. I went to the sink for a sponge.

Billy said, "I'll go and see Auntie Alice and Uncle Mac tomorrow. I'll get them a present. I'll tell them something. You go to bed."

I wrung out the sponge in the sink. "What are you going to do now?"

"Spose it is too late. Watch telly a bit."

"There's some of yesterday's pie in the fridge. Why do you do this to me?"

His head was sunk and shaking. "Sorry, Mum. I couldn't help it. Honest."

"None of the bloody Roberts can help a bloody thing."

I left him and went to bed.

I couldn't sleep. Drink sometimes has that effect on me. I either go out like a light or I'm as dry as dust, and in that rotten state where you are tired but wide awake. No matter what I tried, I couldn't switch off. I was worried about Billy and didn't know what to do. It wasn't possible he had a system, a nineteen year old boy. I don't believe in magic.

I thought of going down to the sitting room and getting a book, but I hadn't heard Billy go to bed – and I didn't want another set-to with him. In another half hour I made up my mind to do it anyway. I put my dressing-gown and slippers on. And I was just about to go downstairs when I heard the front door slam.

It must be Billy. I looked at the clock – it was nearly three-thirty. He wasn't going up the Grapes at this time? That would be disgraceful.

I ran downstairs and out the front door. I looked for Billy down the lamplit street. I couldn't see him. He must have rushed off to the Grapes. Then I turned in the other direction, and there he was, squeezed into the hedge, walking quickly, a few hundred yards up.

I didn't think about it, I just followed after, keeping in close to the shadows. He hadn't taken his car, so he couldn't be going far. That made me extra suspicious. Normally people with cars drive down to post a letter.

He cut through a side street, and I had to run in case I lost him. My slippers kept coming off but I managed to keep him in sight, as I huddled in close to the fencing. Then past the derelict prefabs, heading up towards Water Lane. I kept my head down in case he should turn, even though I doubt he would know it was me.

A man was coming towards me. I scurried on to the other side of the road. He walked past watching me. I glanced back. He was standing there still looking. I hurried on. Only madmen, murderers, and Roberts come out in the dark.

On Water Lane I couldn't see Billy.

The road was clear, the shops shuttered, a single back light on in the chip shop. A car came from somewhere and went somewhere.

I crossed over. Just down the street opposite was the alley behind the shops. The alley was in pitch darkness, but I knew it must be where he had gone.

I began to walk along it slowly, leaning in against the wall. It smelt of dustbins and damp, and was earthy underfoot. I could hear a baby crying.

I all but struck the door, but pulled back at the last instant as I saw the glimmer of light. It was open. I listened. I could hear a faint scraping. Opening the door as little as possible I slid in.

Instantly an alarm went off and I froze in panic. Then there were footsteps running and a swinging torch, and someone rushed into me throwing me to the ground. I glimpsed a shadow that went out through the door, and slammed it shut.

The alarm went on and on. In the scuffle whoever it was had dropped a few things, including the torch which was still alight on the ground. I picked it up and shone it around the room I was in. It was a betting office.

I tried to open the back door but it had obviously locked and couldn't be opened without a key, or a skill I didn't have. I walked through the foyer of the betting office, the alarm going on and on like a scream. I tried the front door. It was shuttered.

There was a strange smell in the place, like pear drops, and miles of brown carpet with thin lines along it like it had just been raked. I circled the torch-beam. High on one wall were big TV screens angled down, like all-seeing eyes. What did they make of this old lady in a dressing gown and carpet slippers? Not the usual sort of customer.

The counter was open. I went through. The person I had interrupted had obviously been behind it. On a table there was a mess of betting slips, and a medicine bottle. In it a liquid with the smell of pear drops. There was a kid's toothbrush lying on a betting slip, with half the writing on it faded out. I picked up the slip.

And recognised what was left of the handwriting. Billy has a funny curl to his h's. So why was he painting out his own betting slip?

It was when I saw the carbon paper I twigged Billy's system. Each slip has a time on it. 3.32 on his – so he must have put a bet on this afternoon for the evening Dogs. Then he went to the Dogs, like he told me, and had broken in to the shop to put the shop copy right. He'd wipe out the losers with that smelly liquid – whatever it was, and then write the winners over the carbon paper on to the shop slip. And tomorrow he'd come in to collect.

So that's what education does for you.

The alarm was giving me a headache. Then it stopped and I felt clearer. I was stuck here until someone came in the morning – might as well make the best of it. I found some milk in a fridge and some tea making things in the back room and made myself a cuppa. I sat on a stool for maybe half an hour, thinking about Billy. He was just as bad as the rest. I felt empty with disappointment. My one hope smashed.

At last I got up. I couldn't leave the mess, with Billy's handiwork plumb in the middle. Going back behind the counter I collected up the betting slips. I put them into a metal waste bin in the centre of the foyer. Then I poured just a little of the smelly liquid over, and threw in a match.

It went up like a bonfire, lighting the whole shop in dancing brightness. In less than a minute it died back into the bin, leaving a sooty stain on the ceiling, and the room heavy with fumes. I went into the back room and closed the door.

There were overalls on hooks, and a towel on a rack by a sink. I took the overalls down and laid them out in a thick layer on the carpet. I bundled up the towel for a pillow, then lay down and tried to sleep.

*

So here I am, on a hard floor in the dark, going over it all. My life with Dan, the girls in Holloway, Johnny who did it his way, and Billy with his system. My beautiful Billy... Oh how that hurts!

How long? Twelve thousand in the bank, a new car... Who taught him to pick locks?

Evening classes?

I sit up, pull my dressing gown round me, and clasp my knees. It's just beginning to get light. I can't sleep. Anyway what the heck am I am going to do in the morning when they open up? I can see the manager, keys in his hands, as he comes through that door for his cup of tea. What will I say to him? What will he say to me?

It's all so ridiculous. Here's me – the one that has always tried to stay out of trouble. The conscience of the family, the reliable one. Whatever we do – don't worry – Mum'll always be there. She'll come and visit us and sort out the kids. She'll be in court when they send us down – and at the gates when we come out. Good old Mum.

Stupid old Mum. Taken-for-a-ride Mum. Used Mum, doormat Mum.

Why should I be so put upon? Why should I be the one that always picks up the pieces? Let the worm turn and grab the bird by the beak.

When they call the law in the morning, I won't say a word. After a day of badgering I'll crack, and explain my system. I'll tell them to look behind the cornflakes packet for my last winnings. I'll say in my statement I have been at it for years, if only I hadn't had the bad luck to be trapped by a new door lock…

I will stick to my story through arrest and trial. Billy will try to say it was him really. Well he would try to save his old mum – wouldn't he? I will plead guilty, and wave at the family from the dock. When I am sentenced I will thank his Lordship.

I'll enjoy being with the girls, and if the food isn't up to much – well at least I won't have to cook it. I've no doubt some of the screws will be unpleasant, but then I'm not expecting a holiday camp. It'll be good for Billy to cook his own meals, but I dare say Alice and Mac will help out. And it will be a relief not to have to go on that train ride to Parkhurst.

When the family comes to visit – I shall enjoy hearing how disappointed they are. I shall make the most of their troubled faces as they ask me the same old question… "Why, Mum? Why?"

"I wanted a rest," I'll say.

Yes – that's what I'm going to do. All the way. From arrest to Holloway. I'll do it my way! My System, Billy.

Except… it won't wash.

The cops'll ask what I did with the money. They'll ask for details of other jobs. And if I can pick locks to get in – why couldn't I get out?

Damn it to hell it won't wash!

I shall simply have to be the confused old lady who doesn't know how she got here. Flapping my arms, rolling my eyes. "I just woke up and here I was, officer."

Let them sort out how I got in.

Let Billy worry about whether they've sussed his system.

But how I wish they'd do me!

The Bangladeshis in the Brick Lane area of Tower Hamlets, also known as Spitalfields, came from Sylhet, in the north east of Bangladesh, and speak Sylheti which has no written language. The first generation who came in the aftermath of Bangladeshi independence in the early 1970s were hard working, rural people, many of whom could not read or write. Some educated themselves and have done well, reminiscent of the Jews who lived there before them. This story was written in 1990.

Business Plan

S YED could not believe what had happened to him yesterday. He'd made over two hundred and seventy pounds selling his light-up yo-yos. In four hours! Normally he worked two weeks to make that much money. And when he was on the dole he didn't get it in a month. Abdul had just given him the lot. "Surplus stock," he said.

What wonder!

While Rebeka was making the breakfast he quietly counted the money under the table. He had given her sixty of it. There was no choice there. You could not ignore a red letter from the Council. He did once, was taken to court, and nearly evicted. The lawyer from the Law Centre had saved him – and he resolved that heat and gas could go – but pay the red letters from the Council.

He felt guilty he could not tell her what he was doing, but she would not understand. She would want the money to pay bills, whereas he had more important things to do.

Talking to Abdul he learned so much, and to think he hadn't wanted to go. He'd gone there like a snail. Rebeka insisted and pushed him, after all the red bills had dropped through the letter box.

Syed had tried one of Abdul's restaurants. And was told he was at his Cash & Carry on Middlesex Street.

Abdul was walking between the shelves smiling to himself as if the items were flowers he had planted. He was portly, his extended stomach held in by a tight waistcoat, over a very white shirt and red tie. Clean shaven and in a smart blue suit, he was the image of the businessman. And to complete it, in his right hand was a cigar like a fuming sausage.

When Syed first knew him he was dressed in rags, a thin, gangling youth. Now his face was full and chubby, with a second chin developing like a cushion beneath the first.

There were two workers in the Cash & Carry, both busy stamping prices on goods and packing shelves. One of them Syed knew slightly, he had worked in the same clothing firm a few years back. He briefly nodded when Syed came in, but returned immediately to his work – obviously intimidated by the presence of the boss.

Abdul recognised Syed at once, and came towards him beaming.

"How are you my old friend? Where have you been all these years?"

"Working and living," said Syed, attempting a smile.

"Yes, like all of us. You remember when we were back in the village? How simple life was then! Of course we had to work hard but none of this worry. I've got a daughter, she's at a finishing school in Switzerland – and the bills she is mounting up…! I told her on the phone I could live for five years in Bangladesh on what she spends on clothes in a week."

As he related his worries Abdul continued to smile, the arm with the cigar spiralling, but never going anywhere near his mouth.

"Then my eldest daughter, she's getting married. What a performance! I would invite you, Syed, but I don't think you'd want to go. The Carlton hotel, and the rows we are having about who should come and who shouldn't, and who will sit on what table. Sometimes in the middle of the night I wake up and think in Bangladesh we would all sit on the floor, so simple. Now it's waiters and place names, and musicians and dancers. We had a whole scene about whether to allow alcohol. Iqbal has lots of English friends from University, and some of my business friends will be coming, and of course they expect..." He threw an exasperated hand around. "I tell you for two weeks non-stop. My daughters insist on a bar, my wife can't live with the shame of it. And I'm thinking Allah help me, let me just take off my shoes and go on a *Haj*..."

He stopped, still beaming and shaking his head. "I think it would be good for them to work in a factory for a few years to appreciate the value of money, instead of just writing cheques and waving credit cards..."

While he was talking Syed had been looking around the Cash & Carry. It seemed to have everything and in no particular order. On one shelf boxes of radios, next to them Christmas crackers, glass jars and fire engines. On another gallons of washing-up liquid in plastic containers next to funny pencil-sharpeners and cuddly elephants. It was like a bazaar, so much, so different. And all of it owned by Abdul, whose family had been the poorest in the village.

Without warning Abdul clapped his hands, startling Syed. "Two teas," he shouted. One of the workers immediately ran off to a back room.

"Last year like a fool I let them elect me to the Committee of the Chamber of Commerce. As if I haven't got enough to worry about... And now I'm in the thick of organising a trade exhibition. Pretty girls in red uniforms, exhibition stands, catering arrangements... I'm thinking maybe we should cancel the wedding and have it at the exhibition. That would be good eh?" He nudged Syed. "My wife's family at one stand, and the groom's at another – all with pinned-on labels."

The thought made him rock with laughter.

Looking at Abdul's shoes, Syed said, "I wondered if you needed any workers."

Abdul drew in close and put an arm round Syed's shoulder, so that Syed could feel the heat of the cigar.

"Hard times eh, my friend? You have all my sympathy there. I remember what that can be like. When I first arrived in this country…" He shook his head, breathing out deeply. "I lived on beans. I mean it, beans. For a whole month, nothing else. I think my daughters if they ate beans for a month…" He stopped, and for the first time put the cigar to his lips, drawing in a deep draught.

"Once, Syed, I employed someone from the village." He exhaled luxuriously. "I won't say who as I'm not one for gossip. And let me tell you the truth, I had to sack him. He was lazy and I think he was stealing. The next year I went back to Bangladesh and he has told everyone what a terrible boss I am. I picked him up out of the gutter, I give him a job – and he's not the terrible one, but it's me, I'm the one everyone says is the villain. His daughter is ill they tell me – did I know that? And can I help it if her father is a thief?"

Syed nodded; Abdul obviously couldn't help it.

"Since then I have said as a principle – and nothing personal in this – I will not employ anyone from the village. And I stick to that like the Koran. Nothing personal at all. But once I start I would be employing everyone – and how could you run a business like that?"

Syed wanted to go now, but couldn't as the tea had arrived. The workman placed the tea on a small table. There was a single chair which Abdul offered to Syed. The workman brought over a second chair for Abdul. When they were both seated, Abdul offered Syed a biscuit from the plate of assorted biscuits on the table.

"I tell you, my friend, you should start your own business. Be independent. None of this signing-on and scrounging. Live well and pay your way."

"My own business?" sighed Syed, sipping his tea. "How can a poor man do that?"

"You have to learn the game," said Abdul. "And then play it better than they do." He broke a biscuit and dipped it in his tea. "When I first came I had rotten jobs. Working in dirty restaurants. I was a slave. But I learnt English, and I learnt to read. So then I could read menus and I could work as a waiter... I learnt the trade a bit, then I got a Business Plan, and with that I raised money and started my first restaurant..."

"What is a... Business Plan?"

"What is it!" Abdul hit the table with his fist making the plate of biscuits and the saucers jump. "It is everything! Without it – forget it. You will never start in business."

"I do not understand..." Syed stammered, unable to voice what he didn't understand.

"Profit and loss, fixed assets. It's all there. Market Research, working capital, balance sheet. All in the Business Plan. And cashflow – every good Business Plan must have lots of cashflow. The more cashflow, the better it is."

"But how...?" struggled Syed. "How does it help you start?"

Abdul placed a soft hand on Syed's. "Money, my friend," he said in an intimate voice. "With a good Business Plan you can raise money."

Syed was beginning to understand. "Ah with a Business Plan..."

Abdul interjected. "A *good* Business Plan. It must be good. No rubbishy, second-rate Business Plan – forget it. Scrap paper." He twisted his mouth to show distaste. Like stretched rubber it formed back into a smile. "I tell you, Syed. In fact I make you a promise, you bring me a good Business Plan and I'll find you the money." He sat back looking pleased with himself. "Now wouldn't that be better than working for me?"

Syed had to admit it would. "Where do I find this Business Plan?"

Abdul brought his wallet out. It was stuffed with bank notes. He took out a card and passed it to Syed.

"My accountant. He does the best Business Plans. Go and see him. Mention my name."

"Will he charge much?"

"Very reasonable."

Syed rose and shook his friend's hand. "I have learnt a lot today." He thanked him for the tea and the advice, and turned to leave the shop.

"Hey – don't go empty handed." Abdul was holding a large cardboard box. "Surplus stock. You have this."

And that was when he had got the light-up yo-yos. When he had opened the box outside the shop he didn't even know what they were. He thought maybe Abdul was just getting rid of some junk, and getting rid of him too.

*

As Rebeka came back into the room he thrust the money into his pocket. She was looking happier. Last night when he had come in she had been so miserable. It was difficult to blame her. All of them living off the little money she made at sewing and the bills mounting up. He had wanted to throw the whole two hundred and seventy on the table – but had given her the sixty – which was sixty more than she had expected.

"Why are you smiling?" said Rebeka.

He tweaked her cheek. "Can a man not smile in his own house?"

"If you smile," she said, "there is a reason for it."

"I am smiling because I have a beautiful wife and a beautiful son."

Rebeka's face softened into a smile. So much better than that dark frown, her reproachful eyes.

"Then why weren't you smiling last week," she said teasingly.

"If I smiled all the time you'd get bored, so I save it for a special day."

She pulled a pile of sewing towards her. "Did Abdul have a job for you?"

"No – but he gave me an address." He rose. "And I must go there at once." He took her hand and squeezed, then put it to his lips.

She laughed pleasantly. "Am I a film star now?"

In the street he thought, I will surprise her. My whole family – I will surprise them all. He put his hand in his pocket. It was so good to feel the bundle of notes. And without that hippy at Aldgate East he might have thrown all the yo-yos away.

Returning from Abdul's Cash & Carry, Syed carried the box of light-up yo-yos all the way to the station. And stood between the landings below the Whitechapel Art Gallery entrance. It was late afternoon and people were beginning to leave work, hurrying down the stairs, and a few coming up. The place was dusty and noisy; the street traffic funnelling down as if through an ear trumpet, to be met by the noise of the trains at exactly the place he stood.

He was sorting out a few to display, when a man in a torn leather jacket came out of the traffic. He took the stairs four at a time, and stopped dead before Syed.

"Oh bugger – how long are you going to be here?"

He was bareheaded, his long hair tied back in a ponytail, and a guitar slung over his shoulder. His face was thin and dirty, teeth chipped and stained. He towered over Syed by at least nine inches.

Syed guessed he was a busker, and also worked out what the man had said.

"Half an hour," said Syed.

The man sighed and flapped a hand. "OK, man." He sat on the steps, stretching out his long legs. His jeans were oily and torn, merging into tennis shoes in the same condition.

Syed took out two of the toys, and holding one in each hand he proffered them at the first passer-by.

"One pound, one pound, only one pound."

The passer-by pulled back and hurried down the steps. Another passed and Syed offered them at the same price and in the same way. Then a flurry of people came down the steps, ignoring Syed and his offering.

"You're in the wrong place, man."

The musician was standing by him as another flurry came down. "Let's have a look see."

Syed shrugged, a little unsure what he meant. The man took the toys out of Syed's hand and began to spin one of them.

"I haven't had a yo-yo in ten years."

Up and down he played it, smiling and shouting out as he increased in proficiency – as if he were riding a horse in a rodeo.

"Yippee – now you see it, now you don't. Amuse your boss, amuse your friends, wow your wife tonight!"

He stopped, and began to fiddle with the side of one of them. On either side a small yellow light went on.

He screamed, "Technology! A light-up yo-yo." He began to play in a frenzy, delighting in the circling lights. Then took up the other, and had the two of them spiralling up and down, around his body. Two commuters drew in from the crowd, dropped a coin into Syed's hand and each took away a yo-yo. At last the hippy stopped.

"How many you got of these?"

Syed indicated the box. The man looked in. "Jeezus – you got a small fortune here." He looked at the two in his hand, and sucked his lip, then said, "Tell you what – you're no good at this. You won't sell any without me. What if I demonstrate and we split the cash?"

It worked like a song.

When they had sold out the hippy suggested they went to a pub to share out the money. Syed didn't like that, but he didn't want to count money in the street, so he reluctantly agreed, and hoped that no one would see him going in. He stayed for as short a time as possible, leaving half of his lemonade.

Today he needed that money. He had come across Brick Lane, down Fashion Street, and crossed Commercial Street into Wentworth Street. There he compared the card with the name on the first floor window. It was the same.

He climbed the dusty steps from the street. They ended at a landing where there was a door with frosted glass and the same name on it. Syed knew it was the door of his destiny.

He went in.

And standing there was Abdul, as round as ever. Today in a grey suit, and it seemed as if with the same cigar.

"Twice in two days. This is a surprise."

Abdul took Syed's hand in both of his and shook it vigorously. Standing by him was a small thin man in a blue pin-striped suit, his hair cut short and with a line of a moustache halfway between his nose and upper lip.

"Nazrul, meet my good friend Syed. You take good care of him."

There was hardly room for the three of them in the narrow office, mostly filled by a desk at which a young woman sat typing with a dictaphone headset over her ears. The scent of her hair lacquer filled the room. It mingled with the dusty hallway smell making Syed feel a little sick.

"So you took my advice so soon," said Abdul. "I'm pleased to see that. Well I must rush. I have to be at Harrods in twenty minutes. Why I have to be there I don't know. They ignore anything I say... I tell you, Nazrul, the best thing is a small wedding. Just the family and a few friends. I could open another restaurant with the money I'm spending... And in the end will anybody be happy?" He sighed heavily. "When my mother and father got married the guests brought the food. The old customs are the finest ones."

He shook hands with Nazrul, who all the time had been standing like a reed bending to Abdul's blast. Then he shook Syed's again.

"Drop in for tea. We must talk about the old times again."

And then he was gone.

The small man smiled at Syed, and addressed him as if he too had known him all his life.

"Do come this way, Syed." He opened the door to his office and directed Syed in.

"Be so kind as to make us a pot of tea, Cynthia."

Syed went into the office. On the window he could see the name in reverse, and could faintly hear the street cries. Nazrul sat down behind a huge wooden desk. The desk made him look smaller even though his chair raised him above Syed. Before him was an old fashioned blotter, and lying on it an old black pen. All the office was old; the ceiling-rose and moulding, the wooden panelling, the shelves, and the boxes on the shelves. As if to say – this is no fly-by-night accountants, we'll still be here when all that plastic is long gone.

"How can I help you?"

He spoke gently, like a kindly old doctor – and yet Syed knew he must be younger than he himself was.

"I would like a Business Plan," said Syed. And he marvelled at the way Nazrul took it. Accepting it as an everyday thing. Such poise, such breeding. The marvels of education.

"Yes, we do Business Plans. It is one of our firm's specialities." He was picking his immaculate nails delicately. Syed remembered Abdul's nails, also clean and manicured. He put his own beneath the desk.

"We have what I call the A1 Business Plan. We use Market Research consultants, full and accurate costings, premises research, two years' Profit and Loss and five years' Cashflow."

Syed breathed in with excitement at the mention of Cashflow. He remembered Abdul saying, "Lots and lots of Cashflow."

"Beginning and ending of course with a Balance Sheet." He was smiling at Syed, who wondered if he should speak now.

"Fixed assets," he said, again remembering Abdul.

"Of course," nodded the young man. Pressing his finger together he went on. "We also do what I call the Medium plan. Mostly done in-house. Book research. Still worthy but of course not the A1. And lastly we have the bargain basement version. Well it's a Business Plan of sorts. And I'm not too sure we should be doing it." He stopped for an instant and lifted his moustache a fraction. "I don't think it does the firm's integrity any good to be associated with it, if I may be frank."

Syed nodded vigorously.

"So now you know what we have to offer – which do you want?"

Syed did not hesitate. "The A1 Business Plan."

The man leaned forward on to the blotting paper, looking intimately at Syed. "I can see you are an old friend of Abdul's. Quality. The best." In English he added, "Birds of a feather." Leaning even further, almost across the desk he said very quietly, "How much are you prepared to pay?" It was so quiet that Syed could hardly hear, rather as if the room was full, and some secret was being said just to him.

He was taken aback, thrown not just by the manner but by the question itself. He didn't want to show his whole hand.

At last he said, "A hundred and fifty pounds."

Nazrul seemed to collapse on the table as if he had suddenly doubled in weight.

Syed quickly said, "Two hundred and ten." Every penny he had.

Nazrul pulled himself back in his chair, as far back as he could go. The smile had gone and his voice seemed colder.

"The A1 can't be done for less than three thousand." He moistened his lips. "The Medium plan at rock-bottom is fifteen hundred, and the bargain basement can't be done for less than seven fifty."

Syed was sweating. He felt a fool. How could he expect a Business Plan for £210? If it was that easy – anyone could have it. It was a rare thing. Cashflow was gold.

Nazrul had gone glum. "How long have you known Abdul?"

"He's from my village."

Nazrul rose and paced across his window, shaking his head and sighing. "What would happen if I did a Business Plan for two ten? I'd have a queue of ragamuffins at my door. It doesn't pay in accountancy to be cheap. You know how much this panelling cost? A pretty penny." He was looking out of the window hands on hips. "I'm not a market trader." Then he turned. "I'm sorry, my friend, it can't be done."

He traversed the room and held open the door. Syed rose, and was crossing to him when the man shut the door and came back into the room, very agitated. He was clenching his small fists and hissing through his teeth.

"Abdul is a very good client of mine." He held Syed by the shoulders. "I'll do it. Give me the money."

Syed took the fistful of notes from his pocket which Nazrul dropped it into his in-tray.

"Two conditions. My name is not on the plan. Strictly off the record – and you don't tell anyone my fee. You agree?"

"Yes."

Nazrul went quickly to the door, his jaw quivering, fingers bending and unbending. "Collect it from my secretary first thing tomorrow morning. Good morning, sir."

Out on the street Syed was mesmerised; he had got it – and so cheap. He was on the threshold of riches. He looked up at the gold lettering and murmured a quick prayer. Just then the window opened and Nazrul put out his head.

"What did you say the name of your company was?"

Syed was speechless. His company? "Syed…" he said without knowing why, then seeing the sign in his mind he shouted, "Syed Enterprises."

Nazrul nodded and shut the window.

The next day he rose early. He had slept fitfully because of his excitement, and Rebeka woke him at least once to get some bedding back.

In the sitting room he paced about. Would he get the A1? He supposed the medium would do, but the bargain basement wasn't worth the paper it was printed on.

It was six thirty. What time did offices open? He knew not seven or eight like clothing workshops. Probably nine or maybe even as late as nine thirty.

Remembering Nazrul's face when he mentioned the price – he suddenly felt depressed. Then remembered that twice Nazrul had asked him how long he had known Abdul, and felt better. Abdul was one of his best customers and he wouldn't risk offending him.

He was between the two moods when Rebeka rose.

"Why are you up so early?"

"It's a bright sunny morning," he said.

She sniffed. "You can't see the sun from this block. You know you were talking in your sleep?"

Syed was startled. "What did I say?"

She smiled, and turned her head teasingly. "You didn't tell me about your girlfriends."

"So what did I say?"

She looked puzzled, her cheekbones lifting and eyes closing to thin slits. "Over and over the same word. But not Sylheti." She struggled with the sounds. "Keshflo, Keshflo. Like that."

Syed laughed. Then looking at her, he knew he had to say something. "It means taxes."

She snorted. "Maybe Abdul tosses all night because of his taxes – but I would have thought my Syed would have something else to think about."

He turned away. How he would like to tell her about the Business Plan – but until he knew whether it was A1 or bargain basement he dare not.

"Why are you so strange today?" she said.

"I am not strange." He moved some knick-knacks on the mantelpiece.

She was by his side. "You're trembling." She put a hand to his forehead. "I think you should see a doctor."

He escaped from her.

"I am a little excited,' he said. "You know the address I went to yesterday…"

"You've got a job," she interrupted.

"Well yes," he said hesitantly.

"Why didn't you tell me?" She was by his side again.

"Not actually a job. A promise. It's a good job. It should be finalised this morning…"

"And then you will pay lots of taxes."

He laughed. And she caught it, drawing up her lips and lifting her cheeks into little dark hills. She brought her fingers to her lips to stop herself. He drew her fingers away, holding the fingertips. He giggled at her, searching her face. Now the two of them – their eyes and lips rippled like matching brooks, without any reason but the presence of the other.

At nine he rushed out of the house, running pellmell towards that first floor shop that held his destiny. Over breakfast each mouthful had oscillated between A1 and bargain basement – and Rebeka was again watching him with that puzzled look. He was glad to be out.

As he crossed Brick Lane, Bosrul called out to him. He waved back and was narrowly missed by a lorry.

"If you get the sack," shouted Bosrul, "mention my name!"

Syed slowed to a fast walk, a little unnerved by his encounter with the lorry. A dead man has no use for a Business Plan.

He attempted to cool himself, to slow his racing mind. He looked into the sky. The sun was shafting between old warehouses and shops, and was spread like a golden carpet on the cobbles.

Syed broke into a run again. There was no stopping him, he must find out. He raced through the back streets and did not stop until he was in Wentworth Street outside the office. There he took the dusty stairs three at a time, and went straight in through the glass door.

He stood speechless before the secretary.

"Ah – I've something for you." She gave him a package wrapped in brown paper.

In the street he ripped it open.

It was perhaps thirty sheets of paper, bound together in book form, in a hard blue cover with a window. A cry of excitement escaped Syed when he saw the name in the window – Syed – and next to it he spelled out "Enterprises'. With mounting ecstasy he flicked through. Beautiful pages of type – and oh figures, pages and pages of figures! Ranks of them like soldiers drilling across the pages.

He ran to Abdul's Cash & Carry, and saw him at the end, seated searching through catalogues.

"Look at my Business Plan!" exclaimed Syed, charging into the shop, holding it before him.

Abdul, at first put out by the charge, settled back into a portly smile. He took the plan.

"That's what I like to see – the eagerness of the entrepreneur." He looked at the cover, felt it as if it were a new coat, and looked back at Syed with approval. "Nice weight. You've got something here. No accountant's name on it I see." He chuckled and winked at Syed. "I think perhaps it's possible to guess who may have done this."

Syed giggled at their shared secret.

Abdul flicked through. "Market Research. The Competition. Market sector. Pricing policy. Sales strategy. Fixed Assets." Nodding away at each point. "Good stuff. Ah Profit and Loss. That looks good. A small profit in the first year, a decent one in year two, and by year five…" He looked up to Syed with a sigh of admiration, "You'll be in Buckingham Palace."

Syed was over the moon at Abdul's approval.

Abdul turned on, then stopped, and in a hushed voice said, "Cashflow." He ran his finger first down the columns and then along the rows. "Year one Cashflow. Year two Cashflow. Excellent! And in summary years three, four, and five."

He turned back the pages, went through them, and turned back again. "Five years of Cashflow. What a business! Down and along it all adds up. Here's the sales, here's the bank balance, the National Insurance… This is better than astrology. Five years of Cashflow!"

Syed was an explosion of joy. There was his Business Plan, his future. Cashflow and fixed assets. Already he knew the words! Now he could tell Rebeka, and would she not be proud!

Abdul closed the Business Plan, patted it gently as if it were a holy book. "Syed, this is the best Business Plan I have ever seen."

"Better than the one you first started with?" Syed asked cautiously.

Abdul waved a hand. "No comparison."

"Will you…" he began the big question, "will you lend me the money?"

"Of course. Should I break my word to a man who I have known from my own village? Rather I would cut my throat first."

Syed could hardly believe what he was hearing. He had the Business Plan, and Abdul was offering the money.

"Not all the money…" said Abdul. "But ten thousand I will put up."

More than Syed earned in a year! A lifetime to save that much. He would always be grateful to Abdul.

"Of course I will only put up mine when you have secured the rest. You understand? An undercapitalised business is bound to fail."

Abdul turned to the front of the Business Plan.

"So if I give ten thousand, you need…" He worked down the page line by line with his finger. "Another ninety eight thousand." He closed the Plan. "Let me shake your hand, Syed, and be the first to wish you luck with your new enterprise.'

They shook hands and Abdul gave him back the Business Plan.

"Now tell me my friend – what are you going to sell?"

I was born in 1943 and have no memories of the war, but as a kid I played on the bombsites with old gas masks and heard stories of the Blitz. My parents were bombed out of their flat in Mile End, and moved to Hackney where I have my first memories. This story is set in Bromley by Bow where evidence of massive bombing brought to mind this story.

Darkest Hour

SURELY this must be the station?

But with the lights so dim in the train, and no lights at all outside, there was no way of telling. Through the condensation on the window Brian wiped a clear oval with his sleeve. It was if he were in a tunnel – he could not see a thing, peer as hard as he might.

In exasperation at the train's slowness he sat back in the seat and squirmed in his collar where the khaki scratched. What would Mum and Dad think of the uniform? The jacket was a decent fit, but he cursed the trousers which sagged at the seat.

It had been his first time away from home; not counting hop-picking, when the whole family came anyway. There had been no honeymoon period, but straight into the bull. Quickly he learnt – don't stand out, and having run twenty times round the parade ground in full dress – don't cheek. He could squarebash, fold blankets as neat as handkerchiefs, and polish boots so they gleamed like flint. The aim, said his mate Nick, was to terrify Hitler with tidiness.

There was nothing out there he could recognise. In front of him two sailors were asleep on the seat, heads slumped on their square-cut collars. They'd rolled on to the train drunk and got drunker with the bottle they passed between them. Their only virtue was they kept the carriage empty. One of them was Scottish and Brian couldn't understand a word he said, the other from Liverpool – and Brian managed to work out they'd just come off an Atlantic convoy. He would have liked to have found out more – but it was useless. They were brash, incoherent and in turns tired and excitable. He was grateful they were sleeping, even though one was snoring, mouth wide and dripping.

Above them, across the long seat, he could just make out three views of Southend. There was one of the pier, one of donkeys on the sand, and the other of shops on the esplanade. Probably the same pictures he'd first seen…when was it? Ten, eleven years ago when Dad won on the Derby and had taken them all to Southend, including Jimmy and Rose from next door. What a racket! Heads out the window, buckets and spades poking out of bags, and a mountain of towels and sandwiches. Funny if it was this same train.

He grinned to think of Mum and Dad at the sea's edge squealing like infants, Dad's trousers rolled, Mum's dress tucked in her knickers, and the kids scrabbling the stones to make a pool for crabs. They collected so many shells to take home that there was a big telling-off before they left, and most got dumped in the station waiting room, except the few that Rose had been collecting. She kept them wrapped in her handkerchief and kept looking at them on the way home, making all the kids sorry they'd left theirs.

The train stopped, the steam breathing like a hard-worked horse. Brian pulled the window down and put his head out. Vaguely he could make out some shapes, black against black.

A voice yelled along the train, "Bromley by Bow!"

Quickly he was out and on to the platform. He slammed the door, and in his eagerness to be away, shut in his jacket tail – and had to open it again and re-close it.

"'Urry up, 'urry up," yelled the voice. "There's a war on."

In the darkness he could barely see the train. The station was shadow, footsteps and muttering voices.

He took what he hoped was the way to the Devons Road exit. He had completely lost any sense of direction. On one

86

side as he passed he could just make out mailbags, like crumpled corpses dumped around the benches. He scraped his hand along and was reassured by the coarse fabric. On the other side was the train, and beyond it the massive blackness of the hospital. So black it was difficult to imagine its activity. He'd been in there to have his tonsils out; impossible to imagine it full of nurses in white and blue, rows of patients in the wards, and their visitors.

It was as if he had come home to a foreign country.

The guard blew and the train hissed in reply. Instantly he was running to the footbridge, hoping this way was the right way. It came into vision when he was almost on it, a darker black, like a proscenium against the deep purple sky. He took the steps two, three, four at a time, the handrail cold and wet. The train was picking up speed as he ran across the boards of the bridge, stopping in the middle, a fraction before the train came through. The dirty, warm smoke blew up his legs, like it had done hundreds of times; a sulphurous tingle that drew him back eight years to short trousers, holey socks – and the gang leaning over the bridge like apprentice train robbers. It was just something you had to do when the train left the station; race it to the bridge. You had to.

It was then he noticed the form, slightly taller, slimmer, that had stopped by him, as he inhaled the smoke like ozone.

"Bri? Is that you?" A high female voice.

He said with caution, "Rose? It's you isn't it?"

"I hope so," she said. He could feel her smile.

"You missed it," he said. They both knew what he meant. The sniff of sulphur was still in the air.

"There'll be another," she said.

"Are you going to wait for it?"

"No. Coming my way?"

He was wary of her. She once was a friend; for treks down the Limehouse Cut with a bottle of water and half a loaf with her older brother, Jimmy. But these last couple of years he had eyed her shyly. They knew too much of each other. And too little.

She took his arm, and they began walking. He felt uncomfortable and a little proud.

"What are you doing here?" he said.

"I'm a land girl."

"Oh," escaped from him, as if he expected everyone else to stand still, while he alone moved on.

"I thought of joining the Wrens," she went on, "but Dad said I'd be sure to be torpedoed off Greenland. I wouldn't mind if Leslie Howard was there…" She chuckled and tugged him. "So then I thought the country life: cows and trees, and shorts…"

"See many short cows?"

"Mostly cabbages."

The ticket man came out of the gloom like a highwayman. They showed him their passes. He grumpily ushered them on.

"What's Jimmy doing?" he said.

"Haven't you heard?"

"No."

"When he finished his training," she began haltingly, "they sent him off to France. Two weeks before Dunkirk. You know?"

He had to ask but from her tone he could already tell. "What happened?"

"We don't know." They walked in silence for a while. He felt he should say something but didn't know what.

Then she added, "He just didn't come back."

"Could be captured."

"Could be," she mumbled.

He'd always looked up to Jimmy. A year older, that bit stronger, that bit more knowing. Jimmy was ginger and curly-haired, with a million freckles. He remembered him coming back after basic training, kitbag over his shoulder, every curl gone. He hadn't recognised him at first.

They continued in a hush to the main road. Jimmy could be a PoW – or he could be dead in a ditch. Brian wondered whether he would get through it. Those two drunken sailors had been going on about torpedoes. Something had gone down somewhere, hundreds drowned or blown to pieces.

Jimmy made it real. Not just the word of newspapers and newsreel pictures. Or even Grandad's stories of the last one. Jimmy was a pal, his age… He shuddered, feeling too mortal. Let me squarebash forever, he thought, as he saw himself with a rifle facing a tank.

At the main road Brian hesitated. He knew the road junction was just ahead – but could see none of it. He could hear the ghosts of the railway yard; the clinking of chains, shunting engines and the squeaking of wagons on rails.

Rose pulled him on just as the siren went.

"I can't stand that din," she exclaimed. "It goes through me like filing metal."

She was stepping out dragging him on fiercely. He searched the sky. It was featureless, lying on them like a heavy tarpaulin.

"I missed all this," he said.

"Lucky you. Six weeks non-stop." As she marched she said, "I thought I'd get away from it as a land girl – but they only sent me to Enfield."

A car was coming, hooting. They were in the middle of the road, and could just see its dimmed lights. They pulled to one side, as the pale lights passed and faded into the gloom.

"Do you think we stand a chance?" she said.

"Search me," he shrugged, seeing a vision of him and his mates shooting planes from ditches.

"I can feel them – just across the Channel," she said. "I think one morning I'll wake up and they'll be here on the streets. Like Poland."

"We've got the Navy," he said.

"They've got the Luftwaffe."

Her pessimism annoyed him. Made him think again of his own chances. He thought of Jimmy again. Jimmy he went scrumping with, Jimmy who bought him his first pint... He wanted her to convince him, not agree with him.

"Half our street's gone," she said.

"Mum wrote."

"Ma Tibbs copped it. They found her in bed, the roof collapsed on her. She wouldn't go to the shelter. Sitting on her savings she was. You know the Bryces at 44?"

"Yeh."

A bus swirled round the corner, its dim lights like the last glimmer of coals on a fire. He could hardly believe it; a bus in an air-raid.

"They've gone to live at Bethnal Green Station," she said.

"Live in the station," he said inanely. "Where?"

"On the platform."

"There's... no toilets."

"It stinks."

They stopped. Overhead they could hear the drone of aircraft.

"We've got to get off the street," exclaimed Rose. "Quick."

A series of sharp explosions rent the air, and in the brief glare he made out the skyline, and above it like a locust cloud – the bombers. He was surprised at his own terror. Throat dry, legs weak, and the world it seemed emanating from his stomach. He had a wild desire to run anywhere, and another simultaneously to lie down and wait.

The explosions were continuous now. Some way off, beyond the houses, there was a sudden ball of fire. Brian counted. One two three... and then a huge explosion as the sound reached them. In the glow he could see where he was. Just up from the parade of shops, maybe quarter of a mile from their street. The ack ack guns began; a booming, as if the sky was a tight skin being repeatedly hit with a hammer.

Without warning they were thrown by a blast. The deafening noise came with the force of it. Brian fell onto his back, and lay gasping for breath. He tried to call for Rose but had no voice. His ears felt strange; he pressed them, poked them, swallowed and sound began coming back in a hiss.

Rose was trying to get off the ground, her mouth open – as if caught in a snapshot.

"Are you OK?" he croaked, his throat burning, stumbling to his feet.

"I think so. My nose is bleeding."

He helped her up in painful slowness. He had bruised his back when he fell, and was still feeling winded. His ears were still hissing as they stumbled out of the road and into the lee of the dark shops. One of them had a door open.

"Go in," she said, dabbing her nose. He hesitated. "Go in," she repeated. "It may have a cellar."

They entered, and trampled across a fallen ceiling, crunching broken glass. He stopped and pulled at her arm.

"Let's get out of here. It may collapse."

"What was that?" She gripped his sleeve.

"What?"

"I heard a cry. Listen."

He could hear the drone of aircraft, explosions, fire engines, big guns and the hissing in his ears. Inside, in the heavy dust – the creaking of the building, and somewhere water pouring. Then he heard it too. A cry.

She headed further into the shop scrambling across rafters and fallen plaster. He followed the sound of her, more cautiously, thinking of the echo that could start an avalanche.

Rose was coughing and choking ahead of him. He made for her, unable to see her in the darkness and dust. He stopped, and struck a match. Only thinking what a stupid thing it was to do as it flared. In the cloudy gloom he made out Rose crouching low in a corner. He went over, shielding the match, tripping over the piles of debris.

She turned to him, he caught her eye and dirty face just as the fire reached his fingers. He winced and blew it out.

"Light another," she croaked.

He did so. Then she moved aside so that he could see; a wooden crate and in it a cat nearly black but for a white patch on the neck like a silk scarf, and by her, five tiny rolls of black fur.

"You take the kittens," she said. "I'll take the mother."

Brian stood dumbly, holding the match, eyes aching from the dusty air.

"Come on," ordered Rose.

"How?" He had lit another match.

"In your coat," she said. "Take it off."

Now he remembered her in their street games. She would order them all about – especially the little kids. And sometimes he would do as he was told, and sometimes stand up to her – eyeball to eyeball, exchanging swearwords and catch-phrases.

The match burnt out. He dropped it. She was unbuttoning his jacket. He caught her hand. She stopped, he stopped, feeling the soft warmth of her. Her other hand came over his. They stood invisible, taking in each other's hurried breath, hands clasped in the dust as the bombs fell. His hand found her cheek. He grasped her hair at the back of her neck and smoothed the down into her collar.

Suddenly he was choking and spitting, and fell gasping to his knees. She too was choking and laughing.

Even with his burning throat he found her hand again.

"Let's get the cats, Bri."

He took off his jacket and lit a match. Placing it down he picked up a kitten. In a snarl of fury the mother threw herself at him. The flame went out as the bundle of frenzy struck him. He yelled as her claws dragged down his hand.

"Bastard!" he yelled, dropping the kitten and thrusting his hand to his mouth.

Rose made a few futile attempts at grasping the mother but was met with claws and snarls. They gave up and scrambled back through the shop. Mother plainly didn't want to be rescued.

"We could leave her some water," said Rose, looking wistfully back, as they came out on to the street.

"She'll find it," he said, his hand throbbing, not caring whether she would or not.

A fire engine rumbled by, followed by an ambulance. Up ahead two people in long coats were running. There was a glow of orange round the rim of sky and a smell of burning everywhere. They walked silently. No longer was her arm in his. He suddenly felt desolate. It would all have to be started again, some other time. If, and when...

They turned into their street. It was immediately obvious everything was wrong. There wasn't a street. There was fire and smoke, there was rubble – but there weren't any houses. Rose was running, then he was: stepping over garden gates, smashed rafters, clusters of brick, broken furniture scattered on the road and pavement.

They stood before 24 and 26. Unsure for a few seconds, but the remains of the lamppost outside 24 confirmed the address. It was as if the two little houses in the terrace had been stamped on by a giant. They were squashed into rubble. There was not a window, not a door in one piece, just a heap of masonry and wood.

Neither could move. They were numbed by the obliteration. The street had been wiped away like writing on a blackboard. Their community of friends, of relatives, of washing lines, of street games, of taps on windows, of back doors – were these heaps.

They scrambled across the remains of the houses and made their way to the yards. By a shattered piece of fence lay the upturned tin bath that he had often enough bathed in, now with a jagged hole in. He picked up a half burnt book; one of his mum's romances...

One shelter had suffered a direct hit and was just a hole in the ground, the other was full of water with a layer of soil on top. No sign of anyone in either.

"Where are they?" exclaimed Rose.

"Oh God…" he began looking back to the rubble of their houses. "Let's hope…"

An ARP warden found them scrabbling through broken china and burnt photographs. The all-clear had gone. Not that they had noticed. The warden said they should go along to the primary school where the survivors were.

Rose straightened up. She threw away the bits and pieces in her hand and tossed her head. "I don't care what's here," she said taking his arm.

There was a firmness in her hold as they made their way to the school.

The A13, or Newham Way, cuts Newham in half. It is a
savage cut because of the never ending traffic, and the difficulty of
crossing it. When it was first built in the 70s, some houses along
the edge were vacated and a wall built to ineffectually block the
noise and pollution.

THE NEWHAM WAY

A fury, a rush of wrath
wrenching East Ham from Gallions Reach,
Plaistow from Royal Docks.
Newham wincing at the open wound,
A slash trampled by buffalo.

Along the walkway, look down,
on the canyon in stampede,
forever renewed,
a continuity of anger, thundering in excreta,
blowing into the dwellings edging the zone;
as they buffer and breathe the loaded breeze.

Dusty, sticky houses,
hands over ears, pegs on noses,
walled in to keep the charge out,
the kids in, but the air floats over the top,
flows down our quieter streets, through windows,
until we become accustomed,
like mice living in landfill.

Many immigrants work in the catering trade. A few have succeeded, setting up their own restaurants and take-aways. Many more have not, getting stuck in the low-waged, long-houred economy. I worked for two summers in cafes when I was 16 and 17, and also worked in a co-operative cafe and bookshop in the 1980s where I spent too long in the kitchen, washing up and cooking. This story was written in 1992.

Cups

L **ARRY** pushed his way through the wood and glass doors, stripping his jacket off. The manageress was standing in the wide hallway, tight-faced, tapping her wristwatch.

"Sorry," he muttered, streaking past to the locker-room. Quickly into his blue baggy overalls, then out, past the manageress again still standing there as if she were directing traffic. Then across the parquet, zigzagging between the tables, and into his domain. And safety.

The dumbwaiter was already full. About him lay the trays from this floor. He heaved himself to it. Lids off the bins. Racks out. Steam was already pouring from the tunnel of the dishwasher. He must catch up. Now that he had got here.

It had been touch and go. When Leila walked out on him during the night he had tossed and turned until maybe half an hour before the alarm went off. But reawakened, sleep was out of the question, he needed a timetable, routine. Work.

Larry went for the trays. Plates in one rack, saucers in another, then bowls in theirs, cutlery, and last of all – but never least – cups.

Always cups.

No matter how hard he worked they never diminished. Plates and dishes had ebb and flow but everyone who entered had a cup. It was like an entrance ticket.

The rhythm of work relaxed him a little. Take a tray, put the dirty crockery and cutlery in the racks, rubbish in the bins. The cups required special care; each had to be pushed down over the scouring brush, which started it swishing. Not one coffee cup or tea cup could be allowed to escape him. Some got off easy, others he ground out in a fierce hatred. Of himself, of the way of things, of cups, damned cups.

Cups in thick white china meant Goodmayes; the institution where, when his being rose up, it could be restrained. God Save our Gracious cup of tea! Land of hope and tea bags!

Here, warm water on his hands, bubbles breaking when he swished the cups, he was safe at least. He peered into the mist of steam, rising out of the entrance to the dishwasher. Hot enough. It was like a long alpine tunnel with Italian engineers digging towards him. They would be disappointed when they met. No champagne – just dirty English cups.

Last night Leila and he had finished off the whiskey before the row. He shuddered in shame; he got stupid when he was drunk, loud, and cringing. Some pathetic beast begging for attention. He nauseated himself.

A rattle of china and metal made him turn. April had come in with her trolley. He indicated where he wanted her to dump the load. She nodded and gave him a sympathetic grin. Her soft black face, like a cushion. It took the blows of life, resettled, and came back for more. He envied her, she had a toughness. Maybe it was a hold on reality. When she sang in the quiet of the afternoon, pushing her slow trolley through the tables, she sang field songs, work songs of her childhood. What was she doing pushing a trolley here?

Once he'd asked her. She laughed, not at him, that wasn't her nature, but at herself. April said she'd come to see the Queen, and when she came in – she would leave.

The first load was set. Larry pressed the button, and the conveyor began transferring the racks into the steam, into the boiling tunnel to meet the Italian engineers. The rumble made him feel a little better. Something was moving, things were going forward. He would talk to Leila over breakfast. Apologise. Suggest they went out in the evening. He would have to borrow some money, but never mind that. First make it up.

He shivered, his mouth was gritty and his teeth plaqued. A tight rubber ring had been drawn around his forehead. It seemed somehow to connect to the broken glass in his stomach. He lifted a tray of piled cups. Brown stains and lipstick on the rim.

No other utensil is like the cup, nothing so intimate. Sucked like a baby at the nipple, or grasped like a whore in an alley. It was left to Larry to wash it away. Clean away that clear evidence of human need. Leave it pristine white for the next hand and mouth.

Leila came in with her trolley, like a nurse in her overalls of red and white check. She gave him scant attention. Like a model of stone and clockwork, her face pasty without her makeup. As she was going out the door she turned to him, held him hypnotically, like a mongoose a snake. Words collapsed within him, and she swept out while he gasped to pick them up.

Putting, emptying, swishing, he pondered the significance of that look, wondered where she'd slept. She was a bitch when she was mad. Concrete-faced, she would make him beg. It had to be done. At lunch he would make a start, his constant wooing. Be nice, no matter what she threw at him. Take it. She'd come round.

A cup slipped from his grasp, and dropped into the refuse bin. Slid into the slops, almost disappearing. He thrust his hand into the warm stew, and drew it out brown with slime; new born from the primeval swamp.

He had to get out of here. Go through the papers. Get something. This mess, these cups, day in day out – it had made him contemplate going home and joining the army. You eat, you get respect; you just have to kill a few people. Could he persuade Leila to come?

And have his children. Get them properly educated, not half educated like himself. But secondary school and maybe college. That was always the thing. Look at his brother – a plastics engineer in the United States. But you had to be educated, otherwise you're just stuck with cups.

Crazy. He was too old for the army. Go home? He hadn't written in three years. What was there to tell them? That Lucy had gone with the kids when he went into Goodmayes. Tea and largactyl. That each day he hung onto, and wondered why he bothered. Life lived. Didn't it? Tea was drunk.

He kept pace over mid-morning. What he pushed into the tunnel, was replaced by what April, Leila and the dumbwaiter brought. Now he must clear it. Make up for lateness, and get well ahead before the rush of lunch. He waded in, and pushed his pace.

At the dot of eleven-thirty he took his pie and chips from Cook and went out into the cafe. The mirrors on either side showed a pinched, dark brown man of indeterminate age, hair thinning, bent forward like an animated hairpin, making his way to the screens across the far end.

Behind the screens half a dozen already sat, thrusting forks. Leila was sitting sideways in a corner, her legs stretched over a chair. Across the table in animated conversation with her was Mohan. Larry took his tea and toast to her, but could get no nearer than the end of her legs.

She ate and listened to Mohan. Larry, as if blinkered, concentrated on his pie. Sunk his teeth into the springy lumps, the hot gravy slipping into his arid mouth, like the first rain on a dry river bed. Slowly he chewed, staring ahead, as if in a station cafe in a strange country. He would show her he could be as hard as she.

But he could not stop himself from listening to their conversation. Mohan was telling her about *The Archers*, who was or wasn't doing what in Ambridge. His knowledge was encyclopaedic. Larry thought, she can't be listening, she is just doing it to annoy. He wanted to turn and look at her. And then rest a hand in hers.

Nausea and anger swept him. The row last night. She was savage; he only wanted to love her; to hold her warm firmness, to kiss her to him – and she bit him. Snarling, swearing at him. Her naked beauty had reared up and become a hissing snake. She threw whatever was handy. Utterly naked, screaming, pursuing him around the room. When he tried to grab her, merely to hold her back, she dug in her teeth until he screeched. When she picked up the bread knife he locked himself in the toilet.

April sat down opposite him. She had opened a newspaper. Good, she didn't want to talk. Larry pressed his legs together, and yearned for Leila whom he could smell, whose shoes pressed him, and whose laughter was torment.

"But it's vital to understanding them," insisted Mohan. "Half the country wants to run a farm and the other half a tea shop."

Larry thought, "I must be somebody. How can I sit here every day as nobody, without respect, without love. Without the power to affect anything." It burst out of him like a desperate fire; his life burning away. How could he get a piece of it?

"Excuse me," she said coldly. She was standing over him. He looked up to her, and held her eyes for a few seconds. Her face was impassive, her eyes glassy blue. He took her hand. She left it between his fingers, lifeless.

"Excuse me," she repeated.

He didn't move. Wondering what she would throw now. Well he was sober, and he could throw as well as she. She maddened and tortured him. Both enraged him and crucified him. He hated her and loved her with absolute pain.

Over him like a totem, her lips curled in disdain. Neither moved. Their tableau stuck, it seemed, for plot. Violence from either would have moved it, but that would have been telling. All the onlookers knew was that she wanted to get by and he ignored her request.

Both remained while the silence screamed. Obscenities of sex, love and self-hatred reflected on their facing mirrors. They destroyed and remade each other, until the manageress appeared over the screens tapping her watch.

Back in the scullery it was as if he had never been in at all. The dumbwaiter was full and being called down for more. Leila and April swept in and out, leaving their loads. Lunch had begun in earnest, and it rained furiously on Larry. Greasy plates, soup bowls, sweet bowls, amidst the remnants of food; egg, gristle, bacon rind, chips in brown sauce, chips in red sauce, chips in mayonnaise, in beans and in vinegar. He thrust the bits into the bins and racked the crockery. All the while the conveyor rattled on, like the goods train to Dachau.

He must go home. Fourteen years since he had seen his mother. In that last photograph she looked so grey and weary. He was half afraid she was dead now. Or would that be saved for his arrival? All of them in bible black on the veranda of the wooden house. He came, she went.

The manageress swept into the scullery. Flushed from assisting Cook in the kitchen, her creased brow glistening, she was the General; supervising lunch as well as ordering, and planning all the tomorrows of the campaign.

She asked him if he wanted to do overtime that evening. He thought long, while she waited impatiently tapping her hip, eager to be fighting Cossacks. At last he shook his head, and she swept out in annoyance.

When Leila came in with her trolley he grasped her wrist.

"Let go of me," she yelled, wrenching herself out of his grip.

"Are you never going to talk to me again?"

She stood defiantly, "I'm finished with you. You're a mad boy." Her eyes darted at him. "You never listen. I told you – but you think I don't mean it." Her body snapped at him like a trap that he dare not get close to. Angry, she was a terrible beauty that frightened and enthralled him.

He cried out, "I love you."

She threw her head back. "I can't help that." And swept out into the cafe.

Larry struggled in a tunnel of pain. Another attempt at love had failed him; like his marriage and his children. Like all those women that came and went, whom he either loved too much or not enough.

His hands saved him. They knew what to do, and did it for him. Eyes streaming, his hands went for this and that, tipped, swished, put this there and that here. Another load came out of the washer as April came in.

She said, "I heard."

He could see her plump overalls, but did not look up to her face.

"Women are like trains," she said. "There will be another one in ten minutes."

He could not speak to her. What after all was there to say? That he was in despair, that there were too many cups?

April took the racks off the end of the dishwasher and stacked them along the wall with the other clean crockery. She lifted with her whole body, she seemed to do everything that way. Sing, clean tables, collect crockery – her solidity was always there.

She said, "Twenty years ago I came on a banana boat. As I came up in the train to London I looked out the window and thought how squashed everything was. There was no room. The sky blotted out by big buildings. I went to a cafe and had a cup of tea, and the woman took my money without looking at me. I got on a bus to go to Hackney and the man I sat next to shifted away. If I had the cash I would have got off that bus and gone straight home."

Larry had stopped working. Arms hung limply by his side, his head drooped.

She said, "You go home."

He shook his head like a stook in the breeze. "I can't go back after all this time with nothing."

April said, "You got your skin. You got your soul."

Suddenly he was blubbing. "I ain't got no soul. I ain't got no skin."

She brought him a chair and sat him down, her large hands on his shoulders. "Then what you got, Larry?"

"I got a pipe to pour down whiskey."

They remained in silence a while. The conveyor had stopped as the last load had come to the end of its run. Larry slumped against her belly and she held him. The beat and warmth of her entered his tears. He was nearly sleeping, not the dreamless sleep of childhood that blows everything away, but the sleep of exhaustion, the sleep after the torturer has done…

His mother was in her rocking chair on the veranda, the grandchildren playing on the path. The patch was full of greenery and orange bean flowers. There was so much sky, its blueness ached. He stopped, hand still on the gate, looked down at his bare feet, at his ragged trousers, and could not move forward. The children played on, ignoring him, and from the rocking chair came the strains of 'Rock of Ages'.

The manageress' voice broke in. "What's going on?" The blue sky broke. The wooden house shattered. The singing stopped.

April said, "He's sick. He should go home."

*

Larry sat on a bench, the river before him, traffic at his back. He wondered at it; how everything moved around you. All with purpose. The river to the sea, the traffic feeding the commerce of the city, even the seagulls whirling into the grey and over the brown empty water.

He wanted a drink, but he had no money so that was simple. He wanted Leila but it was clear she didn't want him. So…

No "so". He must move too. He was part of the eternal movement. Food, shelter, and the escape of loneliness. Earlier fate had dropped its cold hand on his shoulder, and no doubt would again. In the meantime he would write a letter home.

No lies. The simple truth.

Prepare them.

How do we decide what to do? I don't believe it's in the stars, but neither do I believe in complete free will. Freud said that in any decision there are at least six people involved. Suppose they are out or in the bath when we need them? No wonder we get things wrong. This story was written in 1998.

Toast

I pick up the phone. "Hello."

I don't like to say who I am as I've had a few nuisance calls and I don't want to give my name to yet another telephone salesman.

"Hello, Tom," says the voice enthusiastically. I can't recall it for a moment, but feel I should, and don't want to ask. "This is Joe Williams," the voice goes on and I've got him. "Have you got a few minutes?"

Have I got a few minutes! "Sure, yes – hang on, can I turn the radio down?" I sprint off and turn down the volume. I can still hear someone droning on so I turn it off. I start back to the phone and see through my kitchen door the pot I have on the stove. I belt into the kitchen, I turn off the gas. Back I rush to the phone closing the kitchen door.

"Sorry about that. I had a pot on the stove."

"That's OK, Tom. You weren't expecting me. So prepare yourself…"

I take a big breath, daring not to think, but I know what I think it is, and why should he phone otherwise? I cross my fingers round the phone wire, cross my legs and wait, breath held, not daring to voice my hopes.

"You've got the job."

"That's great," I say. I want to yell and scream, run through the streets naked, but that is not the image I want to put across. I am cool, calm – to my new boss at least.

"You know the conditions and salary?"

I do. Big, fat. I am amazed I got this one. How I exaggerated at the interview! I had taken my thin experience in ergonometrics, and fluffed it out like a soufflé. It would only have needed an apt question to show it was just hot air.

A sudden thought impales me. Did I turn the toast off? I closed the kitchen door after me and so I can't see. I know I turned off the beans. But what about the toast? I had two slices under the grill. Did I or did I not turn it off just now?

"So do you agree, Tom?"

"Yes," I say automatically. I haven't heard a word.

"I'm surprised at that. You led me to believe you might have been sceptical."

"I have reservations," I say.

How long before the toast burns? Then what would happen? It would burst into flames, and the flames would leap out of the grill and catch the oil pan. Can cold oil catch? It would depend on the heat of the flame. The pan is dirty, oil on the outside… It would lead the flame in like a fuse.

"So that's settled then."

"Right," I say, my voice hot and shaky.

"You don't sound so sure."

"I'm sure," I say. "Never been surer." I am trying to look through the wood of the door. How long before the smoke starts appearing under it? Would the fire brigade come in time? How would I get out? What about the people next door? They've got kids.

"So three thirty. OK."

"That's fine. Three thirty is fine by me."

It's a two hour fire door, I think, or is it half an hour? Surely I should smell the smoke? Depends how hot it is. There'd be sounds, plates cracking, wood buckling… The kitchen cupboards will go in no time and fall off the wall. The lino will bubble and flow and burst into dirty black flame.

"I'm pleased to have you on board, Tom. I won't say any more. We can talk it over at the office when you come over."

"Fine."

"You seem a little worried."

"Excited. At getting the job. It means a lot to me."

The sooner I can phone the fire brigade, the sooner they will be here, the sooner it'll be put out. The sooner I can arrange my life. Thank God I've got the job, I'll need a new kitchen. My credit cards are in there! Where's my glasses?

"Bye, Tom – look forward to meeting you."

"Goodbye, Joe – thank you for phoning."

His phone goes dead, I slam mine down. I take two strides to the kitchen door, am about to rip it open, and I stop. Never open the door. I saw a film once about a group of people in Hackney playing cards. They saw smoke under the door, one of them opened up, and the flame rushed in and engulfed them. In a second. Thinking about it I wonder how the TV people knew, seeing the only witnesses were burnt to cinders. But this is no time to cast doubt on the veracity of TV documentaries, mind you some of them do make you wonder, especially the fly-on-the-wall ones. Would people really say all those things with the cameras watching?

I feel the handle. It isn't warm. I get down on my knees and dog-like put my nose to the bottom of the door. I sniff along the edge. Smoke sinks, or does it? No, idiot – it rises, I've seen bonfires. Not until the room is full will it seep under the door. That sounds right. There are times when you want things instantly confirmed. I could check on the internet. World Wide Web – Smoke.

Should I phone the fire brigade?

And suppose there isn't a fire? Three fire engines tear down the road, sirens blaring, ten burly men, six foot three in their stockinged feet, smash in the front door, charge up the stairs… I'll be done for nuisance. False pretences. Stupidity. I'll be in the paper. My new boss will read it. The secretaries will laugh as I walk by.

But I can't just wait out here, until smoke starts pouring under the door. I have to take charge, make decisions, show I am the man who deserves the job. What did I tell them at the interview? "I am great in a crisis."

I run down the stairs and open my flat door. I take a look back up the stairs – is this the right thing to do? There's a fire extinguisher in the kitchen. Probably red hot. I take the few steps along the hallway and open the street door. I step out and absently push the door behind me. As it slams shut I realise I am outside without my keys. The woman downstairs is at work… She'll be back in about two hours, just in time to see her flat ablaze. It might burn up that damned cat of hers, screeching on my rooftop, chasing pigeons. But she has a cat flap. Unlike me, the beast doesn't need a key.

My kitchen is on the first floor. I can't see too well what is going on in it. I back off, down the path, onto the pavement, then between the parked cars and into the road… My neck craned, leaping up to look. A hoot makes me jump back onto the pavement. I wait until the road is clear and cross over and look into my kitchen. I have a blind covering the bottom half of the window and net curtains over the top half. I hate being stared at. I know it's bourgeois; nets and blinds are common. My last girlfriend and I had this big fight. I won, she moved out. Well it wasn't quite cause and effect. Let's say an element in the sex war. If she were still with me, she'd have the spare set of keys. But she spent hours in the bathroom and could never be early for anything.

A sudden crack and the glass pops out, black smoke billows from my kitchen window, red and yellow flame brushes the woodwork…

I want to dance and sing. My house is on fire! The relief I feel at the knowledge. I could call the fire brigade now and be treated like a regular human being. On top of that I have a new job. Oodles of cash. I can get a new sound-system, computer. I'm seeing the boss at three thirty… Three thirty when? When?

"Has anyone phoned the fire brigade?" says a woman. For the first time I notice there are other people watching the flames leaping from the window, now licking the eaves of the roof.

"No," I say.

"Someone should. That could burn the whole house down. In no time. Catch next door too. They've got kids."

Three thirty when? I had agreed to see him – but when? Was it tomorrow or the day after or next week? I had said – yes fine, no problem. He has a high opinion of me. I came over as confident and organised at the interview. I haven't had the offer letter yet. It's not official till you get the letter. They can deny phone calls. I can't just phone him and say – when did you say? But wait a minute – he's got a secretary! That's the way. I'll phone her and ask her to confirm the date. I'll start with something chatty, after all she'll be seeing me around from now on, then I'll say as a sort of after-thought – *could you confirm the date and time I've arranged to see Joe* *– I have half a feeling I'm double booked*. No that's no good; double booked is incompetent. I've been mugged, my filofax has been stolen. My dog chewed my notepad, my hard disk has crashed…

"Do you know who lives there?" says the woman. I note she is wearing a red headscarf. Quite peasant-like.

"I live there."

"You insured?"

"No." She is on the young side of middle-age, plump with green eye shadow, the hair poking out of the headscarf is too black to be really black. "Can I use your phone?" I add.

"Sure."

I follow her into her house. She has left the door open. We go into her spotless kitchen. I notice she has a toaster. If only I had had one…

What is Tom's telephone number! Heck! I don't know it. It's in the flat, in the sitting room. How will I phone his secretary? Three thirty when? Is it a half hour or two hour fire door?

I am holding the phone, the woman is looking at me strangely.

There's nothing else for it.

"I'll phone the fire brigade," I say.

Earlham Grove is a street of two- and three-storey late Victorian houses, near Forest Gate station, where I have lived since 1993.

EARLHAM GROVE
Forest Gate, E7

Builders came with the railway line,
navvies moved on, porters on platforms,
horse buses ambled to the City over half a morning,
but the train, the rip-roaring stallion, steamed
into the soot of Liverpool Street in half an hour.

Houses for comfortable families of five or six.
A little sniffy, to show which step of the ladder.
Servants to live out, housemaids you have no idea,
and keeping a good cook in West Ham!
Layers of brick, solid as the Empire,
respectable as a Queen thirty years in mourning.
Bay windows with a glimmer of classical,
pretend pillars at the door, a little ornamentation
under the windowsills, repeated round the portico.

Red polished stairs, shinier than the neighbours',
smoke rising from chimneys, baker respectful at the
    door,
horse snorting at the kerb, maid gasping at the
    mangle,
mistress seething at the stains on the antimacassar.

The beautiful take the prizes. How unfair! Isn't being beautiful enough? And the ugly – well who defined them as such? Need they be grateful too?

Ugly Fruit

I T was mid afternoon. There were few people in the cafe. She didn't like it much, it smelt too strongly of frying and tomato ketchup. The tables were too small, and they'd crammed them too close. Nor did she like the way the Italian waiter kept looking at her.

But Jeff still might show up. Knowing him.

She took out his photo from her handbag. Handsome bastard. That smug look. She remembered the first time she saw him at Christine's party – and couldn't take her eyes off him. That childlike innocence. An illusion of course, but scrutinising the photo she wondered what it was that made him so handsome. His nose wasn't special, the shape of his face ordinary. His lips were exciting but only because she knew them. In a photo-fit she wouldn't pick them out as sexy. He had good teeth but so do lots of people. Deep-set, beautiful eyes – but aren't most eyes beautiful? They reflect light. His curly straw-coloured hair, longish, and arrogantly untidy. None of it special. But put it all together and he was a stunner.

Not that he said he was married. Wouldn't have told her at all but she saw him with a young boy outside the swimming baths. So after a little shameful following, the quizzing of a neighbour – she had the evidence to confront him, and to spoil several evenings. Most likely today too. She put away the photograph and glanced at her watch. 21 minutes late.

It had begun to rain and the cafe was filling up. She had no wish to move and ordered a second coffee and a sandwich; not that she was particularly hungry or thirsty. Just somewhat abandoned, and here she could buy her place.

She stared at the window, watching the droplets roll down and join up, listening to the swish of traffic. Would she phone him? And be accused of nagging again. He would eventually phone her: tomorrow, the day after, next week – who could say? Would she go jelly-legged and cave in again?

No. She was adamant.

A man came and sat opposite and she resented the intrusion. Her view of the window was cut off. She glanced at him and almost winced. He was one of the ugliest men she had ever seen. She turned away but held the vision of a bulbous nose, a cratered face, and two large bays that ate into his wiry hair.

The man shifted in his seat, folded his umbrella and splashed her in the eye. She cried out and jerked backwards.

"Sorry," he said.

"S'all right. It's only water." He handed her a napkin. "Thank you."

"I didn't realise how wet it was."

"It's all right," she said, a little exasperated. "I'm OK now."

She put the napkin down and couldn't avoid his face. Heavens, he was ugly, but she couldn't look away without being rude. He couldn't help his appearance.

"Don't give you much room these seats," he said. "Do they?"

"They don't want you to stay long," she said, taking up her cup and sipping. It was too hot but she held on for protection.

"What shall I have?" he mused, glancing through the menu.

She wondered whether to leave, though she still had a full cup of coffee and an uneaten sandwich. Not that she owed this man anything. She could go when she liked. Let him think what he wanted.

"Waiting for someone?" he said.

"No," she said quickly, having no wish to tell a stranger she had been stood up. He wiped the droplets on his cheeks round his face. She wondered why he didn't grow a beard to hide the pock marks. Was he married? Would anyone have him? She rather doubted it.

He caught her looking.

"I know what you're thinking."

"What?"

"How ugly I am."

"I'm not."

"You don't have to lie."

A waiter stood at his shoulder, the Italian one that had been staring at her. Did he think they were friends? Lovers perhaps? The man ordered a pizza and tea, and the waiter left.

"You're all the same," the man said bitterly.

"I beg your pardon."

"Women," he hissed. "You'd spit at me if you could."

She held up a hand. "Please stop."

His mouth twisted. "Why?"

"I am not women. I am *a* woman."

He grinned, his teeth yellowish, irregular. "A representative of the breed anyhow."

"Thank you," she said coldly, clutching the cup tighter, a compound of anger and guilt.

"If only you would leave me alone," he exclaimed.

"I didn't start this conversation," she retorted.

"You did."

"How?"

"The way you looked at me."

For a second she was silent, wanting to justify herself. She sipped her coffee and stared at the sandwich. She didn't want him to watch her eating.

At last she said, "You needn't have sat opposite me."

"The cafe is crowded."

"There are other places."

"This one has the nicest view."

A smile escaped her.

"That's better," he grinned back.

"You do have a cheek."

"I don't have much to lose," he said.

The waiter came with the pizza. He gave her a sniffy look as if she had gone down in his esteem. She saw it and gave a short laugh.

"What's up?" said the man.

"Oh, just something I was thinking."

The man began eating the pizza, she munched the sandwich. Suppose Jeff had been here, she thought – then what would have been the waiter's reaction? That she was classy. But instead she was the dregs. Desperate. Well he was half right.

"I'm in traffic," said the man. "The lights at the junction have gone awry."

"I've noticed old ladies scampering across."

"They try too hard to keep cars moving," he said prodding a piece of olive. "Most of them with one person in, polluting the planet."

"A car is a convenience," she said. "Especially for women."

He gave a scornful laugh. "I hate women with cars."

"More than you hate women in general?"

"Much more," he said as he forked a large piece of pizza into his mouth.

"I've a car," she said.

"Then I hate you even more."

"You are devastatingly honest."

He suddenly leaned forward, putting a hand on the table close to hers. "What are you doing tonight?"

She spluttered her coffee, crumbs spitting across the table. Apologising, she wiped herself and the table.

"Your chat up technique…" she said, calming down. "It takes some believing."

"Why?" He was not eating, but glaring at her.

"You said you hated me."

"I do."

"Then what makes you think I'd come out with you?"

He gave her a thin-lipped smile and sat back. "I was preparing for failure."

"Setting yourself up for it, more like."

"You mean, if I hadn't said I hated you, you'd have come out with me?"

She didn't reply. The irony struck her; she was being given the run-around by a handsome man, and here in exchange was the beast. Could she save him from his consuming hatred? Might he not, in a few weeks, be intensely grateful to her? As an alternative to her Greek god who could pick and choose from among the nymphs... It was just... She was ashamed of the thought. He was eating his pizza, looking down at his plate. But the thought swelled out again. Could whatever fantasy, thought, chemistry – make her ever want to kiss that face?

Jeff's ear she would take anytime, plus whatever was attached. Yet she knew she didn't like Jeff. Needed him, yes, but like him – no. In this she could understand the beast. He was despised by what he wanted, women. So he hated them. In a milder way she could see it was happening to her and Jeff. Except for her there were other men; fairly soon she could re-enter the lists. If it all wasn't so wearisome, and all the good looking men weren't pigs...

"I'm sorry," he muttered, "thrusting my problems on you."

"Don't worry about it."

"I should learn to be polite."

"I understand," she said.

"Do you?"

"I think so."

He sighed. "When I was a kid, I always hoped that one day... there would be someone, somewhere, out there for me."

Someone as ugly, she thought, but did not say.

"But everyone I fancy, doesn't fancy me." He laughed bitterly. "It's a cosmic injustice."

She hardly knew why she said it. Perhaps pity, perhaps guilt at her limited view of beauty, or simply bravado. "Where were you thinking of taking me?"

He shrugged uncomfortably. "I hadn't got that far. I assumed I was wasting my time." After a pause he added, "Was I?"

"That depends what's on offer."

He gazed at his nails. "The pictures."

"What film?"

He looked at her helplessly. "I don't know what's on."

"Find out."

He stared at her, searching her out. "Are you teasing me?"

She didn't reply.

"Because if you are…" he halted, and in that warning she saw the danger in him. In his stiffened jaw was no longer the beast that could be tamed but the one that swore vengeance. She felt her heartbeat raise, her breath come quickly… She had to get away. She had offered too much.

"I don't take kindly to being teased," he hissed.

"Let's forget it," she said anxiously.

"I won't," he snarled. "Bitch."

It was then Jeff came through the door, water splaying from his ringlets. A throw-away smile on his lips, barely aware that half the cafe was watching him.

She at once rose to greet him, throwing her arms round him.

"Where have you been!" she gasped.

Jeff gazed at the man. "Is he bothering you?"

She shook her head, clutched at him like a life-ring and directed him towards the door.

The man watched, as in a blast of air the couple left. The door swung shut. The pock-faced man stroked his cheek and finished his tea.

For a working class child, going to Grammar School was like getting a free ticket to the middle class. The other side of the coin was the division it could create in the family, and alienation from the community. This story, written in 1990, is set on a Tower Hamlets Council estate. At the time over 80% of the borough's housing was owned by the Council.

The Daughter's Visit

NOBODY has to live like this, thought Gloria as she parked the Volvo by the pramsheds.

It's not simply money. Look at the rubbish on that patch of grass. When she was a child it was green and clean, and weren't they worse off then? The pramsheds were locked up and the area in front clear. Now half had their doors smashed in, and the space in front was a general tip.

The place had no pride. Which meant the people had no pride. Where had it gone? She remembered polished steps. Housewives would scrub the stone in front of their doors. Why this squalor?

She was afraid for the car. They would make it match. The spirits here, the vandal spirits, were waiting for her to turn a corner to scratch it, kick it, rub it with their dirt.

Two boys were playing in a broken car. One was driving and the other sitting on the bonnet thumping the metal with his fists. The windows were smashed and the wheels had been taken off. The rear seat, lay on its back by the boot.

She walked across, the high heels of her red shoes clicking on the tarmac. The two boys looked up and watched her approach.

She stopped a little way from them, having second thoughts. Two scruffy ragamuffins. She looked back at her Volvo: it shone like a jewel by the wreck of the pramsheds. She could see them rubbing it with mud. They lived in mud. Mud people.

"Would you like to earn a pound?" she called.

117

In an instant they were off and out of the car and standing beside her. Hastily she took a step back, not wanting to touch them.

"Stay there."

Clipping open the catch of her crocodile handbag, she rummaged in with a leather-gloved hand. Took out a pound coin, which she held up between first finger and thumb.

"One now."

The boys came forward. She stepped back again, and closed a gloved hand over the coin.

"If… you look after my car."

"Yes, miss." Wide brown eyes in a dirty face, the collar of his check shirt ripped. The other plainly Asian, his darker colour disguised the dirt of his skin, but not of his clothes.

"Another when I come back." She handed over the coin with minimum contact.

"Yes, miss."

She indicated the car. "Mind you watch it."

They nodded vigorously. Such easy money.

As she wandered off the two boys stood gawping. When she turned round a little later they were fighting, rolling over and over on the tarmac. She knew she should have given them two fifty pence pieces.

When she saw the playground Gloria wanted to cry with rage and disgust. It was covered in shards of glass and everything was broken. The swings, where she had played, were the corpses of swings. The wood on the roundabout was smashed, deliberately smashed, and the metalwork rusty. It was a charnel house of a playground.

She left as quickly as her tight skirt would allow, and took the first stairwell. She would walk round the balconies to the flat.

Stepping into the lift, she at once stepped out, overpowered by the stench of pee. The foot of the stairs was a scrawl of spray paint. 'West Ham' competed with 'Paki bastards' for the lion's share, the spaces between taken up with ornate signatures.

Bare concrete stairs echoed to her footfalls. Light drained from hexagonal openings that she knew once held glass. No doubt the Council had given up replacing it – and taken it out once and for all. Gloria stopped at the second floor. Her mother lived on the fourth, but only the second floor balcony went all the way round the square.

Before she went to grammar school she had played 'Knock down Ginger' with the other kids – up the stairs and around the balconies banging all the knockers. Their rampaging and screaming caused fury amongst the residents, especially those on the second floor where the balcony ran right round. The eleven-plus stopped her street games. Grammar school said goodbye to her friends from the flats. There was an unspoken agreement. She knew she had climbed away; they knew she had become a posh kid.

Each day she would come in and out in her gym-slip and straw hat, face stiffened in non-recognition as she passed old friends on the stairs and balconies. At first she had to work at it. Soon it became natural. Like the Latin declensions she learnt. By the third year she knew more about the lives of the Romans than she did about the teenagers she had once played with.

She worked hard at keeping school and home apart. Gloria had never once invited a school friend home. For a start few lived close by as the school was at Mile End, two stops by tube. But mostly because she could not bear it. The flats would shame her. Her parents would shame her. Horrible things – like toothbrushes over the kitchen sink. And the dripping her father put on his bread.

There was still washing along the walkways as she clipped by, all these years later. Past alternate blue and yellow doors, a window on each side, demarcating the flats. About a quarter weren't occupied. Plywood sheets covered windows and doors, as if the residents had been boarded up as plague victims. Apart from the empties, there was one innovation since her time; each door had a spy hole.

How many original residents were still here, apart from her mother? It was a theoretical question. The last thing she wanted was a door to open and her passage be interrupted. Not that it was likely; she had retained her grammar school technique of not seeing.

At the end of the balcony she rounded the corner and came to that strange architect's folly; the triumphal arch between the first block and the one parallel to it, with the walkway running over the arch and into the second floor balcony of the other flats. It was probably meant to add a little grandeur. Sort of Woolworth's Le Corbusier.

Now there was talk of taking it down.

In the middle of the arch she glanced down at her car, and the two boys playing with a ball nearby. That would be an irony, if she had paid them to shatter her window. She shrugged; what could she do?

The last flight of stairs. Stairs that still entered her dreams. Anyone could be on the stairs, and there sometimes was. At the corner, where they met the triumphal arch, heavy petting went on, at least that, while she worked on Latin and trigonometry. Even as a girl she rarely used the lifts. Frightened of being stuck in them, and the alarm telling all and sundry. But perhaps more frightened of the encounters. She could ignore someone on the stairs by simply looking straight ahead. That was difficult in a lift.

The wind caught her hair as she made her way along the fourth floor balcony. Down there the regiment of pramsheds and the patch of ill-used grass. Each footstep struck a nail of memory. How long they were, those grammar school years! And what glee she felt when she had been accepted by Nottingham to study Botany. The letter she had carried round for weeks, reading and rereading it with ecstasy. She knew she would never live here again.

Gloria rang the bell. While waiting she looked at her watch; one twenty-three. She would give herself two hours. Three twenty-three was her absolute limit.

120

A policeman answered the door. The flat-capped sort, red pinched face, rocking on his feet.

"Yes?" Only his lips moving, staring at her with opaque almost fishlike eyes.

"I've come to see my mother," she said, her eyes and voice registering her anxiety.

"Ah," nodded the policeman. A policewoman in a sleeveless blouse put her head and arm out of the back room.

"That the daughter?"

The policeman nodded.

"What's wrong?" said Gloria, pushing down her alarm.

The policeman scratched the side of his nose and came in close. In an intimate voice he said, "Your mother's been up to her tricks again."

Gloria covered her face. The trials of an only daughter. She knew there had been something when her mother hadn't arrived.

"Where is she?"

The policeman indicated the back room with a shake of the head.

Gloria stepped in, squeezing past them both.

"We'll be off then," he said. "She's appearing in court in the morning."

All at once Gloria felt like a tree blasted in a storm. Exhausted, felled. She flapped an arm at the departing officers who closed the door behind them.

Her mother was seated by the gas fire, one foot on a footstool, the stout leg covered in thick brown stocking, creased at the knee.

"Hello, dear."

Gloria took a wooden chair and brought it forward. She dropped on to it. There was a stale smell in the room, so familiar she knew it instantly. She turned to the horsehair sofa, tufts of hair poking out as they had always poked out. And no doubt beneath its cushions and in its crevices she would find treasure trove; coins and hair slides, little plastic games.

"Tea?" Her mother had risen.

She nodded as her mother limped into the kitchen, the same faded paisley housecoat. It must have been bought faded.

The tiled mantelpiece was a clutter of knick-knacks; a barometer, some dusty coasters, cotton on wooden cotton reels, a pin cushion, a fork, a small china terrier and a postcard of Weston-Super-Mare. At the end the shelf took a step down. On it was a schoolgirl picture of herself. Pigtails, plump face and a show of bright teeth, above a white open-necked blouse. In dust and memory she felt no older.

Her mother was shifting in the kitchen, sounds of tins and china. In there she had done her homework, on the red formica table with the drone of the TV from the sitting room.

This morning she had known there was something wrong. Her mother always came by taxi on a Thursday morning. Gloria paid. When she hadn't arrived, Gloria had tried to phone, only to find it out of order; she was left with little option but to go over.

Her mother was coming from the kitchen, the cups and saucers clinking in her hands, tea spilling into the saucers. As she tried to give Gloria her cup she spilt more, until Gloria took it from her, taking in as well a dry smell of incontinence. Her mother put her tea on the arm of the chair and eased herself back into the sofa, breathing heavily.

Gloria tipped the saucer back into the cup. The cup was thick white china and dirty with fingermarks. Gloria opened her lips to complain, and then shut them again. On her list it ranked too low to bother with, and she lacked the energy to even begin.

Her mother's breathing was subsiding. How did she get about, Gloria wondered? With frequent stops no doubt. And if the lift was out of order... how long to climb four flights?

The old woman brushed back her wispy hair, a gold wedding ring biting deep into a plump hand, and veins like twigs impressed on the back. Her face was puffy with drooping cheeks, and pale blue, watery eyes. Her bushlike hair was receding a little at the front.

"How's Graham?"

"Fine."

Graham didn't like her mother, which was why after her father died she had timetabled Thursday mornings. That was duty done with no fuss at home. Home being Hornchurch, not here for a long time. The children also didn't like their grandmother much. Her presents were tatty which they didn't mind when they were little, but as teenagers, with the allowance Graham gave them, it was not what they expected. Mostly her gifts went straight to a charity shop.

"And the children?"

"Benjamin is starting a new school. It's more expensive but he wasn't getting on well at the last one. Ruth only has time for her pony."

"I bought her this."

Her mother searched down beside the chair and came up with a book, obviously secondhand, with a picture of girl embracing a horse.

Taking the book Gloria said, "She'll probably like it." Knowing she wouldn't. It was too secondhand, too young, too her mother.

She sipped a little tea and watched her mother sipping hers, blowing it as she did so. All that was needed was her father in the other chair in his socks.

At last she said, "Why were the police here?"

"When?" her mother said, eyes shifting nervously.

"Just before."

And waited in the dusty silence as a slow, closed lip smile formed in her mother's face, drawing in her cheeks and lightening her eyes. If only Gloria had had brothers and sisters to involve in all this. Everything was thrust on her, since father died five years ago.

"It was all a misunderstanding." She sighed and waved her arms. "They don't listen. I kept telling them."

"Who?"

"All of them. The shop manager, the woman, the policeman… I told them all."

If it had been one of her children Gloria would have followed through immediately. None of this rambling nonsense. But in her mother's space, with the photographs, knick-knacks and brown furniture, the confidence she had at home evaporated. There, firm, authoritative. Here, a schoolgirl.

Weakly she said, "What was it you took?"

Her mother licked her lips rapidly and pulled her head into her chest. "It was only a little thing."

"What?"

"Oh a little thing. They have hundreds of them…"

Gloria closed her eyes. Through the wall she could hear faint pop music, and over it her mother's breathing. Did it matter what it was? All that mattered was that it was. Then she snapped. Reason disintegrated, and a shriek burst out of her soul.

"For God's sake tell me!"

The harshness of it pushed her mother back into the chair. "Just a battery," she said in a frightened voice. "Only a car battery."

"A car battery?" repeated Gloria, and questions crowded out any sense. "Why… how? A car battery?" She pulled in her scattered thoughts. "It's heavy. However did you manage it?"

Her mother indicated her wheeled basket in the corner by the door.

Gloria groaned. She could see her mother pulling it like a recalcitrant donkey. "Why a battery?"

"For the car."

"What car?"

Her mother sat up and looked at her as if her reply had been as plain as day. "Your father's car."

124

"He's been dead five years."

"You think I don't know that?" Her mother pushed herself up as she spoke. "You're not the only one with brains."

Her mother was on her feet and making her way slowly across the room, her steps small and laboured. It was then Gloria had a flash of recognition. If she turned she would see her father at the table, eating egg and chips, wiping up the egg with his bread. In shirtsleeves and collarless shirt, off from his shift on the railway – a dirty newspaper propped up against a mug of tea.

She turned. The two chairs were pushed quietly under the table, asleep like a pair of ancient dogs.

"There," her mother was calling from outside. "There."

Gloria hurried out. Her mother was standing on the balcony by a dead tomato plant pointing over. "There."

Gloria looked down at the wrecked car. "Daddy's car?"

Her mother nodded. "I was going to fix it. As a surprise."

Back in the flat she quietly told her mother she mustn't steal. If she wanted anything she only had to ask. Gloria would willingly pay. Stealing wasn't fair on her, on Graham or the children. It embarrassed everyone. She said the same things over and over, wondering what her mother was thinking, as she nodded and said she wouldn't ever again.

At three twenty-three Gloria rose.

"I'll take you to court in the morning."

"No dear, you don't have to. I'm sure you're busy…"

"I'll be here at nine."

Leaving the flat on her way to the stairwell she could feel her mother at the door, watching her. As if Gloria were a toy with a spring attached: she could only get so far and spring back.

When she got down to the courtyard the two boys ran up to her, gesticulating.

"We tried to stop 'em, miss."

"They wuz too big."

She wept over the car, shamelessly. It was sunken on one corner where the tyre was flat. The two boys stood around sympathetically, giving her details of how they had tried. The Asian boy showed a bruise on his face.

There was no jack. She searched the boot over and over. There was nowhere it could hide but she looked again as if her need would make it reappear.

The boy with the torn collar said, "Johno can fix it easy."

She continued searching the boot, while they ran off shouting, "Johno! Johno!"

No jack, and no magic to make one. She slumped sideways in the car, door open, tapping one of her heels on the rim. How would she explain this to Graham? Supposing she ever saw him again…

Johno was a burly man in baggy jeans and pullover that didn't quite make it to his waist, the area between a proud crescent of beer gut. He had a tangled mass of rusty hair, and, more importantly, a tool box.

As Johno worked away the two boys assured her that he would do it. Johno could do anything. "There's nuffink he don't know about cars."

Which may have been true, but Johno didn't have a Volvo jack. The car rose a few inches, then fell off the only jack he had. When it had fallen three times she went to look for a phone.

The first she found was vandalised. She walked on and around, asking and following the directions indicated. There was a long way between phone booths. The streets had changed considerably since she knew them. The old terraced houses gone and been replaced by estates. Estates that had been born and grown old in the time that she had been away. She walked through them with a feeling of panic. She shouldn't be here. She had left, got out – why were they holding on to her like this?

Women hanging clothes on balconies, children playing in the courtyards watched this well-dressed woman, obviously lost, tracing and retracing her steps in a labyrinth of memory and housing blocks. They could not see the child who had played five stones on the steps with her friends – round

126

once, round twice, boysie and girlsie – before she was kidnapped by grammar school.

In despair Gloria hailed a taxi.

"Hornchurch."

As she left in the leather womb, her panic eased away. But not her despair. Her car and her mother remained at Bromley by Bow.

At the time of writing, the Olympic village, post Olympics, hasn't yet become housing as the changeover continues. It will be a vast estate, and such places in the East End have often become awful places to live in. I hope this poem is unduly pessimistic.

OLYMPIC VILLAGE

Picking up needles with rubber gloves,
appealing to teenagers smoking dope by stairwells,
"Why not try the youth club?"

For 17 days, ten thousand runners, swimmers,
cyclists, wrestlers, basketball players
in flats without kitchens,
oscillated to the excitement of commentators,
medals, tears, anthems and flags,
sponsored by McDonalds and Coke,
came, competed, bye-bye, on to the next meet.

Men and women with black bags and brooms,
on minimum wage, bin tissues stained with sweat,
blood and make-up, plastic bottles for beer, water
  and shampoo,
soap, toothpaste, tampons, forgotten sponges and
  flannels.
Beds and tables ferried away as builders return,
kitchens added, more floors, carpenters, electricians,
  painters
bumping into each other like Keystone Kops.
2,818 pristine flats.
Ballyhoo and bunting for the opening.

They are replacing smashed lightbulbs,
putting condoms through letterboxes,
offering another amnesty on knives and guns,
thinking, why didn't Paris get it?

As we get older we become trapped in who we have become. Responsibility treads on our dreams. But every so often a chance is offered. Dare we take it? This story was written in 1986.

The Case of the Hackney Man

8.05 am. Glancing at my watch, I held in my stomach to control my breathing. I had run from the station and just stopped before the door. I felt like a crushed leaf. I'd been up half the night with Sharon who was teething. The only thing that kept her quiet was walking up and down with her over my shoulder.

Wiping my thinning hair forward I entered, to be instantaneously greeted by Mr Taylor, shirt-sleeved in his glass office. "What time do you call this?"

No point saying five minutes past eight. Mr Taylor would just take that as cheek, and cheek for Mr Taylor was rebellion. Only last week poor Charlie – who used to have the desk opposite – had answered, "Time I had a raise."

"Get your cards," said Mr Taylor to Charlie. No point saying there hadn't been cards for years. Mr Taylor, a podgy, red-faced man, like a lobster just drawn from the pot, didn't like to be told.

I entered the sanctum and mumbled an apology, knowing it was useless, but for form's sake. In front of him were columns of figures that he was running up and down, not giving me the merest glance. He was always there before me in the morning, always there after I left. Maybe he stayed all night. Where did he sleep? Did he sleep?

"Five minutes a day." He picked up what used to be Charlie's calculator. "Times 365 days, minus weekends, minus 24 days holiday. That's..." His fat ringed fingers prodded. "That's 19 hours and 45 minutes of my time every

131

year." He slapped the calculator on the desk. "Shall I take it out of your holiday?"

Part of me wanted to laugh even as I cringed. Not real laughter, more like hysteria. He was waiting like my very own devil, poised over my account. On the debit side 19 hours and 45 minutes. Payment requested in 30 days.

I began the litany; trains, baby, wouldn't happen again. It wouldn't have been like this if …

"Don't waste more time," he screamed. "Get out there and find those builders!"

9.02 am. At the site. Where are the builders! The bane of my life. They're never where they should be. Always ready with a hundred excuses. Charlie used to deal with them. He had a way. Rough and ready but they respected him. Me, they think I'm a wally. I've heard them say so when they thought I was out of earshot. Lose your temper, said Charlie. Walk around with a pickaxe handle. So I did – and Stan, the one with his zip always down, asked me if I wanted any help finding my head.

The house was open. Wide open – and no one there. Anyone could have walked off with their tools, the electric cable, the plumbing, the wash-basins, the bath. They don't take a blind bit of notice.

The job should have been finished last week. Mr Taylor's got tenants waiting to move in. Hallway full of floorboards, flex sticking out of walls like worms poking out of rotten apples. Rubbish all over the yard, down the hallway. How can anyone work in a tip like this?

Hysteria rising again. I just want to walk off and go sit in the park; watch the bees and the gardeners hoeing. Each morning like this, so close…

If we didn't have the mortgage. If Joanie wasn't three months pregnant and Sharon didn't grow out of Babygros every six weeks…

9.34. Stan and Tubs turn up. Stan's smiling at me. I know he's got a smart one. Smart enough to save me from Mr Taylor?

They have found a body.

They'd come in first thing and taken out the rotten boards in the back room to lay concrete – when they found it. They were that shocked they had to go off and get some breakfast.

Naturally.

I went to the back room, tripping through the rubble in the hallway. The room was stripped of boards and rafters. I stepped down into the space, like into a pool. There in one corner, picking up the little light from the shuttered windows, was a skeleton.

The feet were towards me, the bones separated. There was something curious sticking up out of the mouth of the skull. I went closer to see. It was a cigarette. I looked behind, Tubs was smirking.

It was too gloomy to make out much detail, with the electricity off. The builders couldn't find the torch so I went off to buy one, grateful for the walk.

10.22. Returned with the torch. Stan and Tubs followed me back into the room, like a pair of sauntering crows.

"Finish off the electrics," I said.

Tubs shook his head. "I ain't working with a skeleton in the house."

It was then I should have lost my temper. "Back to work or get your cards." Like Charlie would have done or Mr Taylor would have wanted me to do. Except I just looked at them. Stan, tall, thin, scruffy and hairy, dressed in old rags, and Tubs short, with a beer gut and balding ginger hair.

They made me feel naked. Their open sneers. I had to do something to show my authority. The White Man's burden, impress the restless natives. This was as bad as the dreadful year I spent teaching.

I knelt down and began to examine the skeleton as if this was something I did as routine. Charlie probably would have got out a stethoscope. The bones were deeply embedded in a flaky rock, rather like a soft slate. I pulled a little off from around the eye ridges. Suddenly I knew what it was.

"It's a fossil."

"Yeh," said Tubs sniggering, "a dead one."

I sucked in my breath. "I think we have come across a prehistoric site."

"You'll find him lying on a West Ham scarf," laughed Stan.

My hackles were rising. Biting my lip I said with all the calmness I could muster, "I want to do a Carbon 14."

"Do one on your brain while you're at it," said Tubs, the two of them cackling like hens about to lay.

I exploded like Etna. Charlie would have been proud of me. I can hardly remember what I said. Things like "cards" and "pig ignorance" and "The two of you couldn't catch a crab with the tide out." How crabs and the tide came into my consciousness I don't know – but like Charlie said: "Get angry, gob in their eyes."

They had both stepped back, rather shocked and rather hurt.

"Finish the electrics," I commanded from the remnant of my anger.

They went. Breathing heavily I wiped the foam from round my mouth.

10.45 am. In my notebook I made a sketch of the skull. I was pleased with it – all considered, in this light and no rubber. It made me feel I could do something.

Carefully with a carpenter's knife I took some scrapings from the skull, put them in a polythene bag and ran to Hackney Station. I took the first taxi in the rank.

11.25 am. I arrived at University College and took the lift to Professor Tawney's lab. I had failed his course four years before. If I hadn't fallen hopelessly in love with a girl in the drama department, and spent my evenings working a follow spot, if I hadn't believed in the Revolution and spent my afternoons in the bar drumming up recruits, if I hadn't slept so long in the mornings that it was opening time when I arose... how different things could have been.

He was at the bench piecing together a few fragments of bone, his thin fingers trembling like a kid with an airfix kit. The professor peered at me through his thick glasses and asked me what I was doing with myself. When I told him he sniffed – as if it had always been obvious I wouldn't amount to much. I told him why I had come.

He jumped up, at the same time drawing his fingers through the forest of his hair and flailing at me.

"Hackney! Did you say Hackney?"

I admitted that I had.

"Wasn't failing anthropology bad enough for you?"

I hung my head.

"That now you have the gall to return with scrapings... Not from Olduvai, Cro-Magnon or Heidelberg but from Hackney..." Further words were beyond him, his jaw opened and shut like a cheap plastic toy.

I stuttered my apologies and began to back out the door. There are times to die. The East London grapevine would be shaking with laughter from root to tip. Stan and Tubs would be in free drinks for a year.

He threw the scrapings back at me. I put them in my pocket and felt my notebook. Dare I show him my sketch? And take more of the professor's scorn... Oh no.

And yet what had I to lose? Wasn't I already the standing joke of the building sites?

"Professor," I mumbled, holding out my sketch.

12.05 pm. Professor Tawney was preparing the bone strips for the gas chromatograph. He was talking excitedly, his shock of white hair trembling like a tree in a storm. His lectures were always visually exciting. I remember him running up and down the lecture hall with the thigh bone of

Homo habilis to demonstrate an evolutionary point, wielding it wildly above our heads as we all ducked away.

12.30 pm. Professor Tawney kissed me! Tears rolled down his red cheeks and held like dew in his moustache as the figures came out of the chromatograph. He danced me round the lab. We broke a glass case, and some paleolithic arrowheads fell to the floor. We simply danced past. He picked up the phone.

"Get me Leakey. Person to person. Olduvai Gorge, Kenya!"

I attempted to piece together what he was saying to Leakey. It seemed the Hackney find was Australopithecus and pre-dated Leakey's by fully 2 million years.

Professor Tawney phoned the Chicago Museum of Natural History, and then the Library of Congress. He put down the phone.

"We must go immediately to Hackney."

1.30 pm. In the taxi he ruminated aloud. If Man had originated on Hackney Marshes, how had he got to Africa – to be found later by Leakey and others? What had driven Man south from the temperate regions to the tropical plains of the Rift valley? Why had Hackney Man then disappeared from prehistory?

He explored a theory of an Ice Age creeping down Stamford Hill thrusting Man and the game he depended on from the Lea Valley (over several million years of course) to the African savannah.

Stopping mid sentence he turned to me, drew from his loose tweed jacket a pocket watch and held it out for me. It was gold on a short chain inscribed by the Academie d'Anthropologie de France for his work on Neanderthal Man.

"For you, my boy."

In my trembling fingers I gazed at it in awe.

Wiping a tear he said, "There will be a Nobel prize in this. Instead of being a footnote to Richard Leakey, he will be a footnote to me." The professor threw his arms around me and clutched me to him.

I sang with inner joy. My life had meaning. Let Mr Taylor stuff his job – what did it matter? If I lost my house – so what? If I, Joanie, and Sharon went barefoot and starving – did it matter a hang? My mother's son had discovered Hackney Man!

2.00 pm. We arrived at the house. It was locked with a note on the door. "Gone to lunch back at 1.30." We sat on the step. In the dust the professor drew alternative evolutionary trees.

"Leakey has it all wrong. As his Australopithecus is only two million years old, he has decided it must be a blind alley, but..." he dug me in the ribs with a sharp finger, "Hackney-pithecus is four million years old and so *must* be a direct ancestor of Man. Or to put it simply, my boy, we have found what the popularisers call the Missing Link."

3.00 pm. The builders return. Drunk. Tubs staggered down the path towards us, his shirt up and his hands clutching his bare belly.

"Taylor's bin," he sniggered. "And Taylor ain't happy with you, boy."

"Get your cards," joined in Stan holding himself up against the gate.

"All for a bag of bones," sighed Tubs in mock sadness as he slid down onto the path, "that wouldn't make a cup of soup."

I prickled with embarrassment for England's foremost anthropologist.

"Give me the keys," ordered the professor, pulling himself up to his full five feet two. "History is waiting."

The builders giggled. Tubs' chin disappeared into his chest. Stan fell into a pile of rubble.

The professor waited, hand outstretched. History outstretched.

"Swun o' them."

3.20 pm. We found the right key. Stan was laid out on the rubble gurgling. Tubs was being a nuisance, offering to buy us a new bone from the butcher. We at last opened the door. The house was in darkness.

"The back room," I said. "I left my torch there."

We ran along the hallway, and through the doorway of the back room. We sank into three feet of soft cement.

As I surfaced from the creamy grit, I could hear the professor spluttering and scrambling beside me. I screamed out for my eyes like a child in the bath.

Before me was a figure. I clawed at my eyes. In my clotted vision was Mr Taylor in the doorway with my torch.

"I wouldn't stay too long if I were you, lad." He played the beam over my face, dazzling me. "It's quick dry."

The car kills thousands a year and pollutes the air we breathe. It gives the illusion of freedom while fracturing society. Where are we going so quickly? This story was written in 1994.

Oranges and Lemons

"WATCH for police cars," exclaimed Stan, hunched over the steering wheel, clenching as if it would fly free from his fingerless gloves.

He was a grizzled man; the hair on his head short and stubby like a brush, almost white. The stubble on his face, though, was pure white. It rasped like a file when he scratched.

Leslie shifted in the cab seat, a spring poking her. The air was soup-thick; of onion, cauliflower, and tobacco from the cigarette that Stan had just put out. She felt itchy and queasy. Drawing herself up the seat she rubbed her knees and rolled her shoulders, eyes flicking rapidly like an engine trying to catch; searching for something meaningful on the bare lamplit road.

They stopped at the traffic lights. Stan fell back in his seat. He stretched his arms to the canopy and let out a long groan that seemed to come from deep in his bowels.

The lights changed. In panic he fell back on the wheel, foot stabbing for the clutch. The lorry coughed and jerked. For a second or two it fought the surge of energy, straining backwards, then gave in like a whipped horse, and settled for forward motion. Stan hunched and stared.

"Police," she said suddenly. It was a lie; she wanted to know what he would do.

"Where?" he screamed in panic.

"Just came past."

In a scramble he moved up a gear and almost stalled. Then the lorry was thrown into a startled charge, while Stan held steely to the wheel, gripped – it seemed – between clenched teeth. Leslie clutched at the dashboard.

"You just jumped a light," she said faintly.

Without warning the lorry turned a wide circle, mounted the pavement, and missed a post box by a thickness of paint. It zigzagged down the side street like a drunken bumble bee. Then a bang, followed by a long scrape of painful metal.

Stan pulled up. He looked to her, biting his lip, childlike, trembling. A tear hung in his right eye. He wiped it away with his forearm, sniffed and opened the door. He paused in the coldness, like a cat sizing a jump, then with a deep sigh he was out, slamming the door.

She heard him running, then silence. She wound down the window and looked out – he was rubbing a long dent in a parked car; first one way, then the other. He did this several times, as if trying to erase it, or push back time. He returned to the lorry, and sat quietly for a minute.

"It's an old car," he said finally.

Then with a tearing grind they shot away. Stan whipped round a right turn, straightened, took a left, then a series of right-lefts which had her huddling her knees, eyes shut. She was fearful he would suddenly let go of the wheel entirely and they would run free like a cattle stampede.

Without warning the lorry stopped.

"Give it a couple of minutes," whispered Stan, slumped in his seat like a old sack. He searched his pockets, and came out with a tobacco tin and lighter.

"Smoke?"

"No thank you," she managed to say.

Stan rolled. Precision and ritual easing his trauma. Tobacco gently placed in the sleeve of paper, stretched, patted into a cylinder – and then the paper brought over in his cracked fingers. He licked the gum and rolled the cigarette between both forefingers and thumbs as if it were a fine Havana. Lighting up, he sucked in like an old chimney pleased to be of use.

She thought – this is stupid. He's mad. Why am I here?

Like one of those dreams where you can't move. She had known it in the market. All the men watching her while she followed Stan as he went from wholesaler to wholesaler. At each one some remark about her. She thought maybe I should go back to hairdressing. This is dirty. Men's work.

Stan had been watching her. He said, "You don't like getting up early – do you?"

"Don't mind." She scrunched her nose.

He had opened his side door. "Come on. Some of the weight's shifted."

They went out into the chilly road. The streetlights were still on, although in the east the horizon was glowing fire. The back of the lorry was awash with oranges. The two of them jumped up and began putting them back in the boxes.

She was cold, sleepy. If she was still at *Hair Today* she wouldn't be up yet. She shuddered. All that fussing with hair. Talking hair all day long. All the other girls seemed to dream hair, had hair on the brain. She had shocked them once by saying she washed hers once a fortnight – if that.

She hated the portraits of smooth, long-faced women with their billowing tresses – and longed to put rude bubbles in their half-opened mouths. But most of all she hated the customers. There was hardly one that didn't suggest a different diet for her. Making her feel like Michelin man. She would inwardly fume all afternoon. In the evening she would go through scenarios where she told them all what's what – having hacked their hair to bits and tied them to the drier.

It was the morning they sent her home to get another blouse that did it. They said it wasn't ironed. Well it was half ironed – and anyway all you could see was the collar over her overalls. Once at home, Leslie decided that she would not go back. She would get a job where no one gave a damn about her collar, and she could be plump if she wanted.

Stan retied the load, then scoured the street for police cars. He jumped off the back and beckoned her to come.

She followed him across the road to a cafe with steamed-over windows.

Entering, they were at once swallowed by an atmosphere of bacon and tomato sauce. It was less than half full, only men, who all glanced up to look at her; that look of disapproval before returning to newspapers and mopping up egg.

Over breakfast Stan said, "Your name. I thought you were a bloke."

Leslie shrugged, both hands round the great mug. "No one said you wanted a bloke."

He ladled his remaining beans on to a slice of toast, then put a strip of bacon on top. Along the bacon he carefully drew parallel lines of tomato sauce and mustard; like insignia for a new shipping line. Folding it as a sandwich, he stood up and indicated the door.

Back in the lorry, the sandwich on the dashboard, he said, "You're a big girl I know, and I seen you hump sacks all right. I mean lucky it wasn't someone on stilettos…" He grinned at her sheepishly.

She gave a little grin back, imagining Jenny from the hairdresser's.

Then he was shaking his head, sucking his lip. "You see, there's just the two of us – you know."

She knew.

She knew, too, Mum and Dad would continue to have a go at her for leaving *Hair Today*. Two years' apprenticeship down the drain.

"Shall I go home?"

He looked at her thoughtfully, biting his cracked thumbnail. "Nah. Stay the week. I could do with help, and I 'spect you could do with the money."

Immediately they got to the shop he drew up the shutters, started Leslie on the unloading, and rushed upstairs.

Stan's shop wasn't big. A wide display that took up most of the shop and splayed out onto the street. An aisle, just big enough for two people to squeeze past, split the display. One half had fruit and salads, the other had the vegetables. Behind the shop was a small room for storage and a toilet.

A little later she was resting up on the lorry back, watching the rush hour; a snatch of music from a car, a woman clattering by on heels meant for a dance floor, a bus with people standing.

Bringing the sacks down to the pavement, she piled them on the barrow. They were heavy but she liked the grubbiness of it. She caught herself in the shop window next to Stan's. Shapeless, rumpled overalls, and streaky face. If the street had been less busy she would have kissed the reflection.

*

Stan helped his mother out of bed. First thing in the morning she could barely move but, once she began, the stiffness eased. She was a little woman, with a creased face that seemed designed to hold her tiny glasses.

In the kitchen he put the kettle on and put her bacon and bean sandwich on a plate, while the old woman settled in her stiff-backed armchair, her side-table loaded with Mills and Boon.

"What's he like?" she called to him in the kitchen.

"It's not a he. It's a she." He brought in her breakfast. "They sent me a girl by mistake."

She sucked in a sigh. "Whatever were they thinking of?"

Stan shrugged.

His mother's head was shaking like a weathercock. "Honestly. I wouldn't credit them these days."

He bent over her, "I'd best be down." And kissed her on the cheek.

As he was leaving she called, "Send her up for elevenses."

Downstairs Leslie stood hands in pockets, trying to sink into them while Stan scowled over the sacks and boxes.

He indicated an empty corner. "New stuff goes there. Otherwise it just goes on the old, and the old goes off. Can you sort it out while I fix up the shop?"

143

She nodded. "Sorry."

He shrugged self-consciously. "I shoulda told ya."

By nine, back and front were straight. Though Stan ran around placing the odd orange, polishing an apple, teasing out a bit of wrapping.

"It's gotta look good," he said. "Grapefruit next to red apples see? Plums next to bananas. Ya gotta see the colour. That's half the pleasure of fruit."

He took her into the back room, and indicated a broken wooden chair. "Now you sit down."

"I'm all right."

His face darkened in offence. "I'm no slave driver. You sit down for quarter of an hour."

She did so.

He went into the front to serve the first customers.

At eleven o'clock he sent her upstairs to have tea with his mother. She was terrified of the encounter. Until a few minutes before, she didn't even know he had a mother.

The stairs came off a separate door next to the shop. A dark dusty hallway and then the narrow stairs. As she climbed she could hear Max Bygraves singing *Tulips from Amsterdam*.

She stepped into the room. For a second the old lady didn't see her. Wrapped in her shawl, concentrating on a book that showed a tearful nurse's face over a mountain, and much reduced, a smiling doctor with an ice pick in one hand and a Swiss fraulein in the other.

"Hello dear," said the old woman, a little surprised. She put her book on the table, and turned down the radio. "Put the kettle on, love. Then we'll have a chat."

The kitchen was small, you could barely turn in it. The kettle was plain metal with a red whistle. She filled it, and searched for matches.

Leslie tried the cupboards, the shelves, the drawers, then went nervously to the front room.

"I can't find matches."

144

The old lady put down her book, and began to lift herself, slowly, painfully.

"No, please," protested Leslie. "I'll do it."

"You won't. I will," said the old woman now making her way across the room.

The stove had a gas pistol at the side. The old woman showed it to Leslie and smiled secretly. "Don't make these now – do they?"

Tea made, she settled Leslie at the table, a wooden oval with a stout centre leg, and a lace tablecloth. The young woman fingered it.

"Is this real?"

"No point keeping it for show." She brought over a tin of biscuits and seated herself in the other chair. "Now help yourself."

Leslie took a couple; the old woman was watching her. She said, "How did he drive this morning?"

"Not very well," said Leslie.

Stan's mother ground her teeth, they slipped slightly, and she poked them back with her tongue.

"One day I think he won't come back. Ever since Dave left..." The old lady stopped. Leslie could feel her searching expression. "Can you drive?"

"No."

The old woman grunted. Then she leaned forward. "He should get a horse."

"A horse?" pondered Leslie.

"His Dad had one." She drew her head over the table, quieter. "Do you think we could make him? The two of us."

"Maybe," said Leslie, thinking that was safe enough. She wouldn't be here long.

Stan's mother put two fingers to her lips thoughtfully. "How would you like to marry him?"

The girl was utterly thrown by the question. The old woman watched her with pursed lips.

"I don't know him, Mrs..." she eventually stuttered.

The old woman waved that away. "You'd have to ask him of course. He'd never ask you."

"I only met him this morning."

"You're a decent girl," she said, "and I won't live forever."

Leslie was recovering from the shock, thinking quickly. The idea wasn't without its attractions. She would get away from home. Never go back to *Hair Today* or anything like it. It opened new vistas. It was stupid.

That afternoon it rained. The two of them sat under the awning between the displays. Stan on an orange box, and Leslie on the broken chair. The rain didn't seem to bother him too much. Between cigarettes he would get up from his box and move the fruit around. He made a pyramid of red apples, then unhappy with it took it down, and began one with alternate apples and oranges. He asked Leslie to boil up the beet, which she did in the back in an old galvanised tub over a gas ring.

Suddenly he called her. She ran out. He was standing over his pyramid of apples and oranges about to put a pineapple on top.

"It'll fall," she exclaimed.

Gingerly he put it dead centre, hands cupped all around. It held.

She clapped. And the heap collapsed.

They ran about picking up apples and oranges. While he put them straight she went across the road for two cups of tea.

Drinking it, eating a red apple, she said, "Why don't you get a horse, Stan?".

He looked at her quizzically. "You bin talking to my mother?"

"She thinks so too."

He fell silent for a little while. She worked on her apple. Then he said, "Where would I keep it?"

She couldn't answer.

"In the front room?" he said. "In the shop?"

The topic was over.

At three she finished. "I don't mind working longer." The rain had cleared.

"No," said Stan. "You started early, you finish early."

She took off her overalls, and put them on a hook in the back, and was about to leave when Stan said, "Take some fruit."

She looked at him nervously.

"Go on," he said. "I don't overpay you."

She took half a dozen oranges.

Next morning Stan's driving was no better. The journey to market she spent cringed in her seat, supposedly looking out for police cars. Returning they had another scrape with a stationary car, before Stan finally stalled the lorry and couldn't restart.

They had to barrow the fruit and veg. There was one barrow on the lorry and another they picked up at the shop. The load that morning wasn't great, but it still took them three journeys. They missed breakfast and worked non-stop to get things ready for nine.

When she went upstairs for her elevenses Leslie was starving. The old lady put down her book. The cover had a tearful nurse in a pith helmet crossing a crocodile swamp with a doctor, lady flier and native bearers behind her.

Over tea Stan's mother said, "Have you asked him?"

"I asked him about a horse," she said, knowing that was not the answer to the question. She told her what Stan said.

"Oh he always says that!" said the old lady. "Did you ask him anything else?"

"No."

"Well you'll have to. He'll never ask you."

Leslie said, "He's given me notice for the end of the week."

Stan's mum grinned. "He's changed his mind."

"What?"

147

"He told me over supper."

Leslie beamed. She was happy. Almost. The old lady gave her another cup of tea and a malted milk biscuit. She absently dipped it in her tea, then looked across guiltily.

"Go on," said the old lady.

As she sucked the biscuit Leslie said, "Do you mind... if I don't ask him... you know?"

"Don't you like him?"

"Well as a person. But I don't know about as a – you know."

"How would you know without trying?"

Leslie flushed, concentrating on her tea. She was unsure what the old lady was suggesting.

Stan's mother said, "I was eighteen when I got married... And four months pregnant with my first." She laughed, her frail hands shaking. "What did I know? You want a trial run? Good luck to you. They got coils and pills now. Good luck to you, my girl."

Leslie was frozen. She couldn't deal with her own thought or the old woman's suggestion. She stared into the tea cup, her face and neck itching.

The old lady said quietly, "Don't you want to get married?"

"I don't know," whispered Leslie.

The old lady's eyes widened. "Are you going to be an astronaut or a Pope of Rome?"

Leslie broke up in uncontrollable laughter, splattering biscuit on the table. When she was at last subdued she offered to clean up but Stan's mum wouldn't let her, and Leslie went back down to the shop.

That afternoon Stan left her alone in the shop. He had to go off and get the lorry fixed. She was nervous, her adding up, although improving, was not as good as it should be. She waited for someone to say – that's not right, dear – probably in front of a queue of half a dozen people. Strangely though no one queried, though she reckoned she was as many times wrong as right.

Mid-afternoon a woman she knew came in. Her hair was thick as a bird's nest, as if it had been recently stolen from the hedge. The woman looked her over.

"You used to be at the hairdresser."

Leslie nodded.

The woman said intimately, "Didn't think you fitted in there."

"Why was that?" said Leslie innocently, holding the woman's change.

The woman fought for words, not looking at Leslie. "Well… you are a bit… casual. Aren't you?"

Leslie agreed she was.

When the woman had gone she looked at her grubby hands. It was good to be casual. Earthy instead of soapy clean, amongst fake smells trying to make out they were garden flowers.

Stan returned later in the afternoon. She should have left an hour before, but she didn't say anything. His shoulders were hunched, arms deep in his pockets. He mooched about sulkily, and then went into the back and began moving boxes and sacks.

She wondered what she had done wrong this time. She went into the back to get a sack of potatoes. He wouldn't look at her. Oh heaven, she thought, I can't cope.

She went to serve the customers. The sums and orders at least busied her. When they had gone, she strode into the back room where he was sitting on a wooden box. She meant to come out strongly – what have I done now? Instead she said soothingly, "What's the matter, Stan?"

He looked to her like a wounded dog. "The lorry," he sighed. "They want eight hundred pounds to fix the lorry."

A ton weight came off her. "I thought you were mad at me."

"Oh not you luvey," he said quietly. "You're a godsend."

She came as close as she dared. "Haven't you got the money?"

He rolled his eyes, shaking his head. "Oh I got it."

She didn't understand at first. "If you've got it…" Then it flashed to her. It was obvious. He didn't want to spend eight hundred pounds on that lorry. Or on any lorry for that matter.

She said, "Let's close the shop. I want to talk to your mother."

In the parlour, the three of them seated around the table, Leslie said, "We *must* get a horse."

His mother nodded vigorously. "The girl's right. I'm glad the lorry's done for."

Stan raised his hands helplessly, and ran his eyes over them and raised his eyes to the ceiling.

"Where'd we keep it?"

"You always say that!" said his mother angrily.

"In the shop?" he said despondently. "In the front room?"

The old lady hit the table. "We'll hire one."

Stan laughed. "It isn't 1930, Mum."

Then Leslie said, "The City Farm." Stan and his mother looked to her. "They've got horses, and a cart."

"Will they hire?" said the old woman.

"I don't suppose anyone has ever asked them," said Leslie.

Next morning at nine thirty Leslie and the old woman set off for the City Farm. Leslie took her arm and they strolled slowly to the bus stop, the old woman chuckling, pleased to be out in the spring sunshine. She pointed out the shops as they went along, saying what used to be there, and what was there before them.

"I liked the trams," she said. "They were solid. Much better than the trolley buses."

"Didn't they jam up?" said Leslie.

"Oh where's everybody going so fast today?" exclaimed the old lady.

They sat on the wall of the Methodist church, while the old lady rested her bones. Leslie suggested a taxi, but she dismissed the suggestion saying she liked the smell of buses.

They alighted close to the farm. The old lady pulled Leslie to her, "You negotiate. I'll chip in."

In the yard a young man was scattering feed to the chickens. A black goat watched as they made their way round a puddle to the office. A tough looking woman sat at the desk. She was wearing wellington boots and a sleeveless jacket.

Leslie said what they had come for.

The woman sat still for a little while with pursed lips, then put her head out the window and called. "Len!"

The young man came in still with his bucket.

"They want to hire a horse and cart," she said.

"Can you handle one?" said the young man.

"My son's drove one for years," said Stan's mum. "With his father."

They were rather set back when Leslie told them it was required four days a week.

"But only for two and a half hours. We'll be back before nine."

The young man and woman looked at each other. Leslie could feel a refusal – but neither of them wanted to be the one to say it.

She said hurriedly, "There's hardly any traffic. We won't overload him. And we'll be back before the farm opens."

The old lady leaned forward. "We'll give you three thousand pounds a year."

Leslie gasped. They had agreed two thousand which was roughly the eight hundred pound repairs, petrol for the year, insurance and etceteras for the lorry.

That did it. The young man and woman said they would have to put it to the committee, and they wanted to give Stan a test – but they could see no reason why it wouldn't be accepted.

Provisionally they could start Monday.

On the way back Stan's mum insisted going upstairs on the bus, and sitting in the front seat. She said, "Tell Stan two thousand."

Leslie nodded. The old lady squeezed her hand. "I'll give them a thousand of my money. I'm not having him again in the lorry."

In the dark of Monday morning, Leslie and Stan went to collect the horse and cart. The horse was a dark brown, shaggy pony called Sally. Stan had had a refresher in handling over the weekend, but it all came back with the first smell.

He led Sally out from the stable. She came as if she had always known them. They gave her a bucket of feed, and put her in harness and blinkers. Leslie simply did what she was told, while Stan talked soothingly to the animal.

When she was secure between the shafts, Stan gave Leslie an apple for her. She held it out at arm's length, and the horse at once went for it. In the show of teeth Leslie feared for her hand, but the thick warm lips barely grazed her as they engulfed the apple.

They hung lamps back and front, as a cock began to crow from the chicken shed. On board Stan placed a blanket across their knees and took up the reins.

When they left the yard he was whistling.

*Back in the 70s the area behind Stratford station was a huge
railway yard, with repair sheds and cranes for loading goods
trains. It was vacated in the 1980s, and became the Olympic
Park for the 2012 London Olympics.*

ROBERT THE TANK ENGINE
*Robert is in Meridian Square, near the entrance of Stratford
station*

By the bus stop, in coat of Colchester Crimson:
a faithful shunter, never on the mainline,
but a backroom Charlie, the unsung engine of E15,
working his pistons raw, grinding his wheels, puffing
the network between the canals and the Lea, assembling
     trains
with wares from the Docks, supplying north and south.

Except Robert is as cockney as a Melton Mowbray pork
     pie.
A substitute, simply the same sort of saddle engine
that shunted loaded wagons round Stratford sheds.
In truth spent his working life ferrying rocks
at the Lamport Ironstone mine in Northamptonshire.
Redundancy forced him south.
What choice does a working engine have?

To Beckton Gas Works, then North Woolwich Railway
     Museum,
which folded in the last but one round of cuts, leaving
     Robert

like a cruelly worked donkey, with no end but the
  knackers,
till Stratford provided sanctuary at the terminus, a
  museum piece,
troubled by a world that has run out of steam.

In the 50s, I went as a child to Saturday morning pictures. Most of all I loved the serials. I identified totally, and agonized through the week how Captain Marvel, Batman or Dick Tracy, whoever the hero happened to be, could possibly get out of the impossible cliffhanger. And on this particular week we were moving from Hackney to Poplar... This was written in 1989.

The End of Captain Marvel

"HE'LL escape. You'll see," said Jimmy.

"How?" I exclaimed.

"Remember Jungle Woman attacked by two crocodiles?"

I remembered. One chewing at her arm, the other at her leg.

"She escaped – didn't she?"

I admitted she had.

"What about Batman and the spikes coming in from all sides?" Jimmy continued, his arms thrashing and eyes wide. "And Dick Tracy hanging by one hand from the cable car? Then remember Flash Gordon climbing the cliff and attacked by a hundred eagles...?" Jimmy stopped breathless and put an arm on my shoulder. "He'll escape. They always do."

The next day I asked my teacher, Miss Hicks, "What would happen if you fell in molten lava?"

Her brow squeezed over her glasses. "Why do you want to know?"

I said I just did. I didn't want to tell her about Saturday morning pictures.

She then told me of her holiday in Naples, and her journey to Pompeii. She sent me to the school library and I wrote this down from the encyclopaedia: *When Vesuvius erupted it covered the island in lava. People buried in it boiled like hot water. When they excavated a thousand years later they found bubbles, which when filled with plaster of Paris showed the men and women in the position in which they died.*

Just imagine being swallowed up in molten lava, your last scream… and a thousand years later – there you are. Screaming. Imagine!

The next day Miss Hicks brought in some postcards, showing plaster people caught by the volcano. I copied some in my book.

Billy, my brother, made the most of it. He said, "Captain Marvel's a weed. Someone was bound to get him. It was just a question of time."

I said he still might escape.

"Not likely," said Billy, and grabbed me round the neck, pulling me backwards over his knee. "Trust you to like someone weedy."

Then Mum came in looking flustered. In an instant Billy released me.

"What are the two of you up to?"

I said, "Billy was strangling me."

She sighed. "Please don't strangle your brother."

Billy looked at his shoes and didn't say anything.

"I don't know why the two of you can't be more help," said Mum looking about the room in a sort of panic. "You know we're moving this weekend. I want the two of you out from under my feet – you can go straight over to the new place Saturday morning. Auntie May will be there. You can help her straighten up as we bring the furniture over."

"In the morning!" I exclaimed. "I'll miss Saturday morning pictures."

"Well that won't hurt you for once – will it?"

Suddenly I was bawling.

She walked out on me saying, "I've enough to cope with. You'll have to get used to it."

For the next few days I wandered about in a sulk. Mum and Dad were too busy arguing and packing to care. And Billy thrived on it.

He said, "It's just films." I knew that. Of course it is. But it's happening. Remember the time the manager came on stage and asked us whether we wanted Dick Tracy to end next week, and we all yelled, "Yes!" And it did.

That proved it was happening *there!* The curtain opened, and there was the screen, like a window to the stories going on behind. It was real, alive, and in our cinema.

On Thursday Uncle Alan and Auntie May came. Dad had gone to the Dogs and Mum was in a state. The sitting room was disappearing into tea chests.

Without warning Mum burst into tears, and Auntie May took her off to the bedroom. Uncle Alan sat with me.

"You down in the dumps too?"

I nodded.

Uncle Alan said, "Well moving does muck you about. You'll be all right once you're in."

I clenched my fist. I didn't give a hang about moving. Captain Marvel was about to be engulfed by molten lava! Moving? Anyone could move.

Then I was bawling.

Uncle Alan said, "What a house!"

I blurted out I had to go to Saturday morning pictures. I would die if I didn't.

Uncle Alan said, you won't die. I told him I definitely would. He bit his nail for a bit, then said all right he'd pick me up after. I stopped crying, unsure for an instant. Uncle Alan repeated his offer. I hugged him – good old Uncle Alan! He smiled like the moon.

I ran around the room, jumping on the furniture, cheering, and Uncle Alan threatened to withdraw unless I quietened down. I did, until Billy came in. Then I did my victory dance again, and Uncle Alan just threw his arms up and went out.

Billy was really narked.

On the Saturday morning, after getting dressed, I went round the bedroom collecting my cowboy and Indian cut-outs. I've been collecting them since before the Coronation. When I got them all together I meant to pack them but I began playing with them. I set the stagecoach up in the middle, had it surrounded by Indians – and then the other cowboys chased along the mantelpiece to the rescue.

Mum charged in. "Get your breakfast at once!"

Her eye was hard. I knew that look. She was ratty and would take a swipe at me. I left the cut-outs and ran past her, attempting to pull wide. She clipped me on the bum. Didn't hurt though.

Billy was already in the kitchen, scraping the bottom of his cornflakes bowl. He smirked at me.

"Yours is drying out."

Mum had come in, and began taking apart the stove.

"You're lucky Uncle Alan and Auntie May are going to pick you up. Just don't be a nuisance. There's enough fuss today what with your father."

I had heard a row first thing that morning between Mum and Dad. Something about money and carpets and the furniture van. I hadn't listened, as I had more important things to worry about.

Mum had gathered up the hot plates and was taking the grill off.

"It would be so much simpler if you came with us."

I had had this argument yesterday and the day before. Best to say nothing, and get on with the cornflakes. I checked my pocket for the shilling Uncle Alan had given me. Sixpence for the pictures, thruppence for sweets and thruppence for an ice lolly. Whew! – it was there. I wouldn't get anything from Mum in her mood.

When I finished I went back into the bedroom. Billy was playing with the cut-outs.

"Leave them alone – they're mine!" I shouted.

Billy flicked over an Indian.

"You're not taking these to the new place are you?"

"Yes I am," I said, and began collecting them together, eyeing Billy who was holding the stagecoach like it was a dirty hankie.

"Kids' stuff."

"Gimme it," I yelled and went for it, while Billy held it high above his head.

"Ya didn't stick it properly. Look at this bit sticking out." He pulled it out further.

"Gimme it." I grasped at Billy's upraised arm, which held the stagecoach six inches higher than I could reach.

"It's mine, titch," said Billy, pushing me away with his free hand, "and so are most of the others."

"They're not. I cut them. I made them up!"

Billy gathered up a handful. "I lent them to you. I'm taking them back."

In a rage I kicked him in the shin. Billy yelled, dropped the cut-outs and threw himself at me. The two of us rolled on the ground, shouting and yelling, until finally Billy came up on top. He settled himself firmly on my chest, and pressed his knees onto my shoulders. Then twisted my nose.

I screamed and Mum came running in. She came straight for Billy and walloped him round the face.

"You're getting on my nerves, the pair of you!"

Billy rose, tears welling, holding the side of his face.

"Get your things together!" shouted Mum. She began pulling out drawers and emptying them on the bed. "Don't just stand there," she yelled at Billy. "Get the suitcases from under the stairs." Billy raced off.

Very quietly I collected the cut-outs and put them back in the cornflakes box.

"What are you still doing here?" she suddenly roared at me. "You want to go to the pictures – then flipping well go!"

I grabbed my jacket.

"Please take my cowboys. They're all in this box."

She grabbed it off me. "Go! Now! This minute!"

*

Me and Jimmy hoped to go up in the circle. After queuing a bit, and getting some kids to keep our place, we went off to buy some sweets. I got lemon ones with sherbet in the middle, and Jimmy got jelly babies. He likes biting the heads off.

When we got back to the queue the kids who was keeping our place had gone in and so we had to go to the end, and finished up in the stalls. Never mind. At least we were in.

I always like it inside; warm, dark, everybody chattery. Long as there isn't somebody big in front. Today there were just little girls.

Jimmy whispered, "I got a flea. Do you want it?"

Before I could say anything Jimmy gave it to me. I didn't know whether it was real or not but just the feeling of it had me itching. Then the programme began, and the flea could bite all it liked.

First The Bowery Boys. Normally I liked them, but it seemed they were just shouting at each other like maniacs. Crazy waving of arms, and I couldn't make out what they were after.

Then the cartoon. Jimmy laughed like a drain. Donald Duck and his two nephews – I never liked them at the best of times. I can't understand a word they say – and now with Captain Marvel at crisis point – how could anyone care about a cartoon?

A cartoon wasn't real.

But Captain Marvel was. Not like Kit Carson fighting the Indians, who was sort of real, but not so real that you could be him. He was cardboard and fell over. But Captain Marvel was a person. Up there, big, in black and white. He spoke, he fought, he flew.

I was Captain Marvel!

That's how I'd get my own back on Billy. I'd say, "Shazam!" and open my shirt to reveal my true identity. And then I'd sit on Billy's shoulders and twist his nose. Then I'd set my conditions.

One – three hundred picture cards.

Two – no more beating up (which Billy wouldn't dare anyway).

Three – me to have all the cornflakes cut-outs from now on.

162

Four – he'd have the window side of the bed.

Five – me to have the soapbox cart…

Or maybe I'd just throw Billy over a cliff and have done with it.

Captain Marvel could do it. In my true identity I could take on the world. One at a time – or all at once. If… the molten lava didn't get him.

Captain Marvel must not die!

If he did, Billy would always beat me up. Would always sit on my shoulders. Would always have the soapbox cart and say the Kit Carson cut-outs were his. Forever.

On the screen it was still Donald Duck, asleep with a trail of jam being followed up by an army of ants. How much longer!

My heart jumped as *The End* flashed up for Donald Duck, and he gave a last wink and squawked at us. Then the censor's certificate for – Captain Marvel!

Oh, say he would live!

The titles, the music – then Captain Marvel flying into the screen. I held my breath.

It started as usual by going back a little way. There was the torrent of lava – and Captain Marvel with nowhere to go but in the cave. There was the lava surging towards him as he backed off, deeper into the cave. Then the sight that I'd been seeing all week: Captain Marvel, back to the wall, horror on his face, and coming for him the tidal wave of lava, about to swallow him forever.

The cinema let out a gasp. I hid my face. It was just as impossible this week as it was last. But I had to look. He *needed* me to look.

"Please please please…" fingers and legs crossed, rocking in my seat like five hundred others.

Captain Marvel jumped. His white ankle-boots coming cleanly together as he took off. There was a hole in the roof of the cave, and Captain Marvel went through, and into the cave above. He glanced back, and then walked out into the sunshine.

It was so quick I couldn't understand it. Captain Marvel had been trapped. I'd seen it a hundred times in my head. The look on his face – total fear. No way out. Captain Marvel knew he would boil like the people of Pompeii...

How could he walk out in the sunshine?

All week he had his back to the wall – and now just a little jump, and the lava's gone. How could that be?

It was a cheat.

Tears were coming. I wanted them to do it properly. Wind the film back and show what really happened. Not suddenly make a hole to jump through when there wasn't one before.

I ran out to the toilet, my face streaming.

Once in the hallway that led to the back exit, I carried on going. I didn't care what happened to Captain Marvel. It was all lies. Molten lava just made you into bubbles.

I pushed down the bar, and opened the fire door. Two boys stood in the white light – one of them I recognised from school.

"Let us in!"

I stood aside and they rushed past whooping. I went out into the sunshine, and closed the door behind me.

The Theatre Royal was world famous in the late 50s and 60s.
The bit of Angel Lane from Stratford Broadway to the station
was demolished in the 70s to make way for Stratford Shopping
Centre.

THEATRE ROYAL

In the market on cobbled Angel Lane, sooty
 buildings,
and a former Victorian music hall struggled in the
 tight 50s,
on my first visit as a child one Christmas.
You couldn't go up in the gallery;
unsafe, the play, the Cricket on the Hearth,
a Dickens disappointment, instead of a pantomime.

Then Joan Littlewood came,
and her Theatre Workshop shook up
that market street, a magnet for writers and actors,
 eager
to get away from dictatorial directors, to make plays
that weren't set in middle class drawing rooms.

On the opening night of Brendan Behan's The
 Hostage,
the police surrounded the theatre as it was rumoured
the IRA would bomb the place.
Shelagh Delaney's A Taste of Honey – well that was
 a shocker,
a sympathetic homosexual in '58, written by a 19
 year old girl;
Fings Ain't What They Used To Be!

In the bar about 1980, a play I've forgotten;
there was a buzz all around,
the barmaid looking over my shoulder.
Dustin Hoffman had come to the theatre,
not for what it was, gone the glory days, but for Joan
with her rollies, cloth cap and the thunderbolt of
   talent.

A friend of mine's family ran a corner newsagent, open until 8 in the evening. Family life went on in the parlour behind the shop, interrupted continually by the shop bell. When the shop closed, his mum and dad went out selling hamburgers from a van. When they stopped work, they went to bed.

Passing Trains

THE milk bottles rattled in the crate outside the shop as Mary took out the newspaper displays. The wind blew up her navy blue housecoat, chilling her bare legs clad only in carpet slippers. She dragged in the heavy bundles of newspapers, each parcelled with coarse string. A single footstep could be heard some way off in the dark street, echoing on the pavements, as if only he and she were alive on this cold, dark morning.

She was a thin, active woman, her eyes continually shifting, restless like she was herself. Needing all the time to be busy, working. The bundles in, the signs out, she unlocked the roller blinds and pushed them up into their housing, revealing the shop window. There was no display in the window any longer. They had taken that down five years ago, withdrawing the dusty toys and knick knacks. You could see the shop itself; the counters, the sweet displays on them and the papers and magazines all around. By the door of shop was the advertisement board. It said, "Rent this space for 20p a week". They had argued whether to take prostitutes' ads. Jack couldn't see why not. If they didn't someone else would. He would put them up, she would take them down. An argument long and bitter without words, symbolised by ads for massage and French tuition. She won in the end as the prostitutes, after first haranguing them for taking their ads down, stopped bringing them in.

Over the railway, beyond the silhouette of house tops, the sky was opening up, a white rent pushing back the darkness. Opening up too her own shutter, drawing her into wakefulness. Taking a deep breath she gazed into the splitting sky. Her sky, her time. Her patch of undisputed ground.

She withdrew into the shop, took the knife from the drawer and began cutting the string with her knobbly red fingers, pushing the blade against her thumb as she cut.

With all the bundles open and against the counters, she began pencilling the papers. One hand scrawled, the other drew away a paper and placed it on the heap, in constant movement as she wandered up and down the bundles.

As she worked her lips moved. She was talking to the paper boys and girls. Explaining to them a running fantasy; Jack had died in the night, but they were not to worry. She would manage everything.

It was light now, and traffic was building up on the roads. Not yet the thickness of rush hour, when it would be solid in both directions. All fumes, and hoots; a crawl of men in shirt sleeves, drumming on steering wheels. A train clattered out of nowhere and went back to it, and then another going the other way – carrying the early workers to and fro. Oiling the sluggish flywheel of the city.

She was still going up and down the bundles when Tim, the first paperboy, came. A tall thin boy, his hair standing on end, face bleary with sleep. He kept rubbing his eyes and yawning, standing there awaiting her.

"Hello, Tim. Is it that time already?"

"Must be," he yawned.

"The usual?" she said without looking up.

"Please."

She went to the counter and threw him a Mars bar, then into the kitchen where she put the kettle on. Automatically she got out six cups, the cocoa, the milk, and made them ready for the hot water. Then she returned to the shop where Tim was loading the rounds into the large, orange shoulder-bags that they used.

Mary sat down and rubbed her back, then massaged her neck, and twisted her head round and round.

170

"How's your mother?" she said.

"Going into hospital next week."

He stopped packing the papers and took a large bite of Mars bar, started to speak but his mouth was blocked with chocolate and caramel, and then thought better of it. He chewed away while she went back into the kitchen and poured out the cocoa.

He called, "I'll have to get the little 'uns up next week."

Mary returned with two cups of cocoa. She gave one to him.

"You'll need time off," she said.

He nodded, taking a large chew of Mars bar and following it quickly with a slew of cocoa. His teeth were streaked with chocolate as he munched and sipped.

"I'll have to manage," she sighed. "Pity it's you. You're my best, you know."

He did.

"It's the little 'uns." He shrugged, excusing himself. "They wouldn't get up or have breakfast if someone wasn't to do it."

"Let's hope your mother gets better soon," she said and gave him her first smile of the morning.

Tim returned it, chocolaty and steamy. This was her favourite time, this brief break sitting on the orange bags, drinking cocoa. And especially with Tim. He was her best; she could rely on him so.

Gill arrived. Plump, freckled, short and whistling. A breathy sound with very little whistle in it, and very little tune. Mary gave her a bar of biscuits and her cocoa.

Gill said, "I thought I was late n'all." Smiling between the braces on her teeth. Her hair was short and straight, like a lampshade. She was good at the deliveries, going out bowed over by the sack but sticking to it. She was not so good at getting up in the morning. At least once a week Mary would take her into the kitchen and threaten to stop her a pound – but she never did, and Gill knew she never would – whether or not it would make any difference. She just had the habit of sleeping through the alarm, as if she were hundreds of feet below ground, below the sounds of the waking world.

Tracy and Bill arrived and joined them for cocoa. Then Eva ran in breathlessly. Mary looked at her watch and frowned, as she handed over the cocoa and Milky Ways.

"Least the weather's held off," said Tim.

Mary kept looking at her watch whilst the youngsters talked of a pop programme they had seen. A last cocoa stood in the kitchen, a skin forming on it.

One at a time they thanked her, placed their cocoa cups on the counters, took up their heavy bags and headed off. She was left with just Tim.

"Bob's a pain," he said.

"Forty-five minutes late yesterday."

"And the day before."

"Shall I go round his house?"

She shrugged, not knowing what to do for the best.

"I could do 'is after I done my lot."

She couldn't believe Tim. He was so good to her.

"No, it's not fair,' she said. "I'll do it."

"I'll see if I can get someone to take it on at school, eh?"

She nodded. A smile of sympathy crossed between them. He hoisted up his bag. She gave him a tube of sweets as he left.

Mary went upstairs. She could hear Jack snoring as she climbed the stairs. She stood at the door of the bedroom looking at him.

He lay in a puddle of blankets, his head thrown back and mouth wide, a liquid rasp coming from him at each short breath. The hairs poking out of his nose shook as his nostrils dilated. He needed a shave. He didn't need a haircut but she knew he would have one. Sometime in the afternoon he would 'pop out'. He would of course go to the pub, and she dare not think where else. Getting a haircut was his excuse for the time he took.

They lived in the same house but seemed to be eternally passing each other, except in bed when she was too tired, and he was sleeping off the half bottle of whiskey he had got into regularly consuming when they came off the hamburger stall in the early hours.

She tore the blankets off him. He lay fragile in brown-striped pyjamas, and pulled his knees up to the embryo position. She shook him, he moaned, she shook him again. He moaned, swung an arm, and relapsed into sleep.

For a moment she stood watching her husband. It was a regular performance. He hung onto sleep like a babe onto its mother's breast. Very well – it was the marbles.

She took the old double-alarm. Loud and rickety, it seemed to shake the whole room when it went off – and she set it for ten minutes hence. Then she took the box of marbles; around two hundred, and poured them onto the metal tray. They lay over themselves in twos and threes like pebbles on a beach. She made space at one side and put the clock down. Then she carefully placed the tray on the mantelpiece.

It was infallible. The alarm would go off, and unless he ran swiftly across the room to switch it off, the clock would shake the tray onto the floor with its two hundred marbles. Once, only once, he had let it go. On getting up he had slipped over backwards on the marble-covered floor and hit his head on the bedside cabinet. He had raged like thunder and needed three stitches. Nevertheless she continued. And now like Pavlov's dog, at the first tinny ring, he would jump out of bed. She could take his cursing; she would get it however she woke him.

Back in the shop a trickle of customers came for their papers, cigarettes, sweets. Very little conversation until around eight o'clock, when people had slept better and had the energy for a smile and a few words.

She heard the alarm, and, very quickly after it, his bare feet padding across the floor, then agonised groaning, and incoherent shouting down to her. Mary winced. There were two customers in the shop, and both looked in the direction

173

of the noise. For them she pretended she hadn't heard, and tidied up the cigarette cartons on their shelves.

The paperboys and girls began returning with their bags, leaving them in the corner. She gave them each their tube of sweets. It was her tiny gesture of appreciation.

"Goodbye, Mrs Maggs." One at a time, a smile through a sucking tongue, and a wave. Goodbye, she would say to each, don't be late for school.

Tim returned. He was always the last as he had the longest round. He grinned at her secretly. It was their unstated agreement. If he was quick on his round, he could stay and browse amongst the comics.

"Jack!" she called up urgently. For reply she heard the chain in the toilet and an incoherent groan. She sighed, looking at the bag of papers still undelivered. She drummed on the counter and called again. She could hear water. He would be twenty minutes in the bathroom, groaning and washing.

Tim was watching her.

"I'll look after the shop."

She hesitated, then looked upstairs and sighed as she picked up the bag. Passing Tim on the way to the door she squeezed his arm.

*

Jack was sitting on the bath, his head in his hands, quietly moaning. Each sound a signal of deep pain, deep despair, weariness. He didn't want to move, he had to move. His head was hollow and banging like a drum. His mouth was raw, tongue thick and ill-tasting.

He rose and sank again, rocking backwards and forwards, swearing repeatedly, and spat in the bath. This seemed to satisfy him a little, and he rose again. Rocked unsteadily as if on the rush hour train, but maintained his balance, and made his way, via the wall, to the sink.

Turning on the hot water, he let it run. Cold water would end the little life he had. In the mirror he prised open his eyes, stretched his mouth, then took out his bottom teeth

174

and pulling down his lower lip searched in the red soreness for the site of the pain. Feeling here, there, rubbing, pushing, pulling, and dribbling down his chin.

The water was hot enough. He put the plug in and filled the sink, then soaked a flannel and sluiced his face. The warmness melted into him, he could feel a little surface life. He repeated it, this time pouring the hot flannel onto this face, and throwing back his head.

He didn't use soap. Washing for Jack was never a means of keeping clean, but for keeping pain at bay. As the heat left the flannel he took in its smell; a stale sweet smell that damp cloth takes on. Removing it, he was there in the mirror again, half a set of false teeth, deep-set eyes, red-veined in a thin, hollowed face with a few strands of hair at the top to be brushed sideways to meet those at the sides. Each day in disbelief at what he had become. This handsome mother's son.

Breathing rapidly, he watched himself – as if to witness that air was indeed going in. At the point of deepest intake he felt a pain in the diaphragm; a worrying pain, but too worrying to see a doctor. Liver? Heart? He was too frightened to be told.

Opening the cabinet he removed a bottle of tablets and poured four into his other hand. He placed them all on his tongue which he held out like a diving board, then scooping water from the basin in a blue plastic mug washed them down.

Step by step, the same each morning, waking up the same way, feeling the same death, and painfully taking the necessary actions to put a little life back into him. In order to poison himself each evening.

Three times he cut himself shaving, swearing like a sailor's whore – and dabbed himself with pieces of toilet paper, throwing the used bits about him, screwed up and red, like dead creatures jumped out of the bath.

Wiping himself as he went, he returned to the bedroom. On the chair was the shirt he had been wearing for three days, each morning the effort to go to the wardrobe too much. Too low in his survival scheme. Besides Mary would eventually change it.

Shirt on, then a tie. Always a tie, that last vestige of his days as an insurance salesman when he was clean, spruce, suited, in a circle of smile and aftershave. The firm's brightest meteor – until he was caught in the park exposing himself to two young girls.

Why, why, asked Mary repeatedly, while he shook his head, tight-lipped.

*

Mary strode, small rapid strides, her wiry body a rush of arms and legs. As soon as she had dropped in a paper, her arm was gathering up the next as she hurried back down the path. She was all rush. She wanted to be back before Tim left.

She loved Tim. She would not admit it, should it ever be put to her. Fond, perhaps, she might have said. But it was more than that. She doted on his coming, his friendliness, his helpfulness. The other children of course she liked, but they never came back to her in the way Tim did. He gave, and perhaps he asked of her – and she was ready to give.

When Joe died, she froze. At least her capacity for love did. She became busy, functional. Moving, always moving – so as not to be thinking and crying. It was a car accident outside school when he was nine. Joe's own fault, running in the road for a ball – and the life was smashed from him. And in its way from her.

From both of them. Joe had made life bearable. Joe was what they worked and strove for. Joe gave them meaning, and their life together its purpose. Now it just went on.

It was about a year ago she began to wake again. Began to respond to the children in the morning. She used to be an old tartar. Sharp, niggly, cross. One morning she was sorting out the papers when she dropped a women's magazine. It opened at a knitting pattern with a picture of a little boy in a grey pullover, tanned and smiling, with his middle teeth missing. He was so like Joe, she collapsed in a sodden heap, and was still there weeping as the children came. Quietly, each telling the next to hush as Mary wept her heart out. When she at last arose they were round her in an awed ring, half sorry, half afraid. She gave them all a bar of chocolate as she sent them out onto the rounds.

It was the beginning of the ritual.

They had been her first tears for years. Since the days of the accident. Like the melting snows in a high alpine meadow; this was her spring. At least the hours of early morning were. Her hours with the children, her paper boys and girls. The dark, crisp hours, secret hours when most of the world slept. She could love again in peace. A love expressed in Mars bars, packets of Polos, and Beano comics.

The streets were busier now; the traffic of the office workers, the first mothers taking children off to school. Older children mooching along, heading for a sweet shop. She didn't like doing a round so late. She would get complaints from those who had left early and missed their paper. Couldn't be helped. Whenever she saw anyone in those houses where she delivered, she called out, "Sorry, I lost a paperboy" – and looked sheepish, but didn't stop for reply.

She scurried. Knowing every house and paper without having to refer to the numbers she had written. She was always filling in for one or the other when they fell sick, or when she was let down. Over the years she had done all the rounds dozens of times.

The last paper stuffed, she hurried back to the shop. Hoping desperately that Jack was not up and Tim would still be there. She would give him fifty pence and a comic, any one he chose. If, oh if, he was still there. He never smiled at her first thing, always so shut in with sleep. It was when he came back from his round, awake, that he was chipper. And growing so tall now, he was almost as big as she was and in so short a time.

177

She wanted to fly over the rooftops. It was getting on. More and more schoolchildren in the streets. Soon he would be joining them if he hadn't already. She began to run. A low-legged run, with her head in front, llama-like. People stared at her strange gait. At her age! She was oblivious to them.

As she came into the shop breathy and flustered, she was hit with ecstasy. He was still there.

Tim got off the stool behind the counter. His face was bright and wide awake now, his upright hair like a paste brush, the rest shaved close round his head.

"Cor have we bin busy!"

She smiled, especially liking the 'we'. His and her shop. Jack didn't come into it. The paper piles on the counter were low and there were gaps on the cigarette and tobacco shelf.

"I had a queue!" He laughed, showing his wonky yellowish teeth. "They just kept coming. Mirror, Sun, Star, 'alf an ounce of this, twenty of that and a packet o' mints."

He had come round the front, and was down to the low shelf of comics, looking them over as he spoke. He didn't bother with the kids' stuff; the Dandies, Beanos, Beezers, but went for the adventures; the zap-pow flying fists and rockets.

"Did you like comics when you were young, Mary?"

For a few seconds she didn't reply. Running back through neglected newsreels of life in the 50s. Life in Bow in three rooms, with Dad more out of work than in.

"I liked the pictures," she said. "If I saved all my pocket money and did odd jobs – I could go every two weeks." She fell into a reverie. The crowded picture-palaces, and some so posh, like the Mile End Odeon; big, grand with pillars and scrolls round the side, and then the flea pits like the Regal at Bow Church with its cheap wooden seats in the first two rows.

"I always remember The Wizard of Oz." She pulled her hands to her face in awe. "When Judy Garland steps out of her house into rainbowland... You must've seen it. When

178

the door opens and colour comes into that grey house…"
She gasped even now at the memory. The girl from dreary
Kansas who had crashed down in a whirlwind, and opened
the door to full technicolor. Mary shook her head, a shy grin
at her silliness.

She knew she couldn't explain it. This generation with
colour TV, born with it, their videos and hi-fis. Her early
years were drab and penny-pinching. And so she had taken
on her mother's dream; a shop. Then you'll always be in
work, said her mum.

Tim was trying to decide between three comics. He
turned to her. "Must be fun owning a shop. Having all this
n'all."

She laughed and tousled his hair, surprising herself at the
liberty of it – but he didn't seem to mind.

"What would you do?" she said.

"Read all the comics." He indicated the shelf greedily.
"Every one before I sold it. When the shop was shut I'd sit
here and read all by myself… All these."

"You can come when you want," she said.

In a low voice he said, "He don't like it."

"Never mind him," she said. "Come when I'm here."

He nodded, then twisted his mouth, a quizzical finger to
it, the nail bitten back to the quick.

"Mary?" he said.

"Yes."

He hesitated a second then it came out. "Why did you
marry him?"

The question threw her back. Such an intimate question,
such a close, clever question. She struggled with her varied
responses – but already it was too late to lie.

"He was very good looking," she began. "He had a way
with him. He was a dresser too. You wouldn't think it now
would you? And beautiful, soft, blond hair." She laughed.
"Don't marry anyone for their looks."

"He's not nice to you."

"I'm not nice to him," she said quietly.

He shook his head. "You coulda done a lot better, Mary."

His cheek cracked her face into a broad smile and chuckle. "Ah but you weren't around then – were you, Tim?"

Tim went red and bashful, pulling his shoulders into his chin. "Gotta go, n'I."

"Take a few comics," she said.

"Ooh can I?" And was already picking them out.

There was a stumbling on the stairs. Tim looked up briefly and said, "See you, Mary," and quickly left the shop clutching his comics, as Jack lurched into view.

He was dressed, hair brushed and a few dried patches of blood on his sunken smooth cheeks. Mary was at the front door watching Tim run pellmell down the road. Jack took the high chair by the till. He was in business.

She turned to him and said, "Good morning." As if he were an acquaintance she saw every day on the way to work, and not the man she had lived with for over thirty years.

"Morning," he mumbled. "Clouding over." Looking through their great front window onto the screen of the world.

"It might rain later," she said, tidying the comics and papers in the racks and shelves.

"Need a haircut," he said.

She nodded. "We should stop this one." She shook a couple of magazines. "Nobody's buying them."

Jack was scanning the newspaper headlines upside down. The scrabbles of black lettering, like ranks of invading armies heading for the sweet rack.

A couple of customers came in. A builder for a Mars bar and a Mirror, a woman for the TV papers. As he served them Mary went up the stairs.

She had been up since five now, having gone to bed at one after closing the hamburger stall. This was her sleep shift.

She quickly undressed – she would not sleep in her clothes – threw on her nightdress and drew the bedclothes

180

over her. She would not waste time, that was sinful – and was soon asleep.

*

In the shop Jack clung on to his stool as if it were the only island in a rising sea. He took the money. He would not move anything, or tidy up, or put in orders. He took the money.

Under the counter he had his magazines which he worked through between customers. Dreaming himself twenty years younger, and wanted by those pouting women.

Or filthy rich. So rich he could buy them all.

Jack had always wanted to be somebody. To be admired when he came into a crowded room. For his money, his looks, his lifestyle. He wanted to be better than his brother in Canada whom he hadn't written to in twenty years. What was there to say?

Approached by a customer he would say, "Clouding over." And must have said it fifty times that morning, even when the sky was thick with cloud. On his stool, one hand on the till, the other under the counter on the page, waiting for the empty shop.

*

Mary got up at one and made herself an omelette. She didn't cook for him. At one time she had, but now he never ate anything till tea time and she got resentful throwing most of his meal away. She then took over in the shop, while he went off to get his haircut.

West Ham Park on a summer's day is a sea of brightly coloured saris and miniature football games. When people-watching, it's evident that amidst all this humanity we stick resolutely to our groups. If we have a group.

Squirrels

MIKE wiped the sweat from his eyes, fingers pressing against the eyeballs. A red glow swirled. When he opened his eyes he couldn't see for a second in the fierce light. Blinking back to vision, he stretched his legs beyond the bench. They were bare below beige shorts, hairy, quite muscular. Age was concentrated above the neck. He could go for 35, he thought, headless.

A family came past sucking ice lollies. Mike licked his lips. Looking across at the ice-cream van, he wondered – no, the queue was too long. Too many kids. When Anne was small he'd send her off to do it. She would run off eagerly in white socks and sandals. Return with two water-ices running down her fingers. These days he was self-conscious, queuing for one ice.

A squirrel was at the edge of his bench. He sat motionless, watching as its tiny paws pressed together as it possessively nibbled a peanut. He could see the rapid beating of a small heart. Beautiful tail, feathery, curved like a bass clef. Cut it off, it'd be a rat. A child approached and the squirrel scampered off across the grass, its back and tail arching in waves. Now it grasped a tree trunk and froze, splayed out as if drying in the sun.

He sighed. It was too hot, here in West Ham Park. And so busy. All these families. Perhaps he should go home, shut the curtains and let the box babble. Babble while it still could babble.

Go where he will, close what curtains he would – he couldn't shut out the landlord.

Two young Asian women passed him, hair black as night. One in a beautiful mauve sari, the cloth flowing with her in gentle billows. Her companion wore bright orange, hair hanging down to her waist. He wondered at the weight of it. It was like a bell-pull.

Suppose he did a runner? This scenario he had played over and over. How could he get his furniture out, his books? Benny downstairs, with the flat off the ground-floor hallway, would report any movements. He was a sort of caretaker. Mike didn't understand his relationship with the landlord, didn't care to ask.

He wondered, could he pay Benny off? What with?

Suppose he packed as much as possible in the car. Then went, radio blaring – like a road movie. But how could he get his things out of the house without nosy-parker knowing? The slightest sound in the hallway and out came Benny's bald head like Mr Punch at the side of the booth.

He licked his dry lips again. He wanted an ice. He wanted to lay on his back on the grass and dream of pleasure beaches. Instead there were nightmares of smashed teeth and broken fingers. Why did he wait? Why had he always waited? At 25 there was lots of time, at 35 time enough, at 55 he couldn't drop the habit. Besides, something always happened. You could reliably leave it to outside forces.

Suppose he left everything? The TV was four years old anyway, the CD player was bought at the same time – when he had a job and was feeling flush. Easy to take the CDs and tapes. The bed, the table and chairs, the sofa and armchair – forget them. The carpets too, the curtains.

Stupid buying that car. A nine hundred pound social security cheque, meant for rent, had bought that wreck. An anguished smile creased his face. He was going to be a mini-cab driver. Except the car went five miles then needed a rest for half an hour.

Bastard lump of metal.

The garage would repair it for £450. Decent of them. Now he had a useless car and owed six weeks rent. He had phoned Anne. Humiliating to beg from your children: her husband Fred had answered. No point asking Fred – so he enquired how everyone was – said he'd like to come and visit, some time, soon – he wasn't sure when as he was busy. Fred said he was more than welcome. Boring Fred. He wouldn't get a penny out of Fred. Always fixing something; new patio, shelves. One day, when he'd done the whole house and garden, he'd make them all coffins.

The next time he phoned, it was Fred again, drill in hand no doubt – and he put down the phone without saying a thing.

He should give it another try. Anne would eventually pick up the phone. Or was that their ruse? It would always be Fred, as if somehow they could sense the urgency in the ring.

A couple sat down at the end of his bench. He pressed away, against the wooden arm. They were in their twenties, lovey-dovey, hand in hand. Giggly; he could hear what they were talking about: a party they had been to last night and how drunk someone was. She was wearing a yellow dress, bright yellow as the water ice. He was in sky blue shorts, Adidas trainers, and a t-shirt for a band Mike had never heard of. They kissed, he cringed and he turned to watch a squirrel watching a little boy, tail like a luxurious question mark.

But the giggling and sighing pressed in.

Fate always intervened. Molecules ever moving. Colliding, repelling, bouncing off walls. Nothing could keep still.

Mike rose. The intertwined couple didn't look up.

He took a few strides away from the bench, wondering which way to go. He didn't want to go home. There he couldn't escape the debt. He hated that house. He must leave. Disappear. Suppose he just didn't go back...? Suppose.

Stuck in thought, he saw he was heading for the ice-cream queue. Kids and mums edging towards the van window with purses and sweaty coins… He was about to walk away when it came to him. It was so simple – he almost laughed out loud.

He would buy two yellow water ices.

It took a long time for the City to move into Spitalfields. Not surprising; timid souls, they are looking for their own sort, and until they are there in sufficient number, they are reluctant. But once they were over the threshold, property prices hit the roof. This story was written in 1988.

Quarter of a Millionaire

I 'M standing by my door in Brick Lane and I'm watching them going in and out of Hymie's old place. For three months I've been watching them bring all the rubbish out, and them coming and going with the fixtures and fittings. Another Indian restaurant. Normally I wouldn't be interested – but it's Hymie's old place. And I told him.

Before the war I told him. I said Hymie you see this area is going to be something. You just hang on and wait. But Hymie went *mshuga*, and goes with his family to Harlow in 1954. I says Hymie you're crazy. You'll work as a cabinet-maker all your life, and you'll never get another chance. Hymie says I'm happy. Which proves he's *mshuga*. I say Hymie you don't know nothing from nothing, just a poor East End Jew – what right you got to talk about happiness? He says money isn't everything. That was more than ten years ago when he retired. I says Hymie if your name was Rothschild I'd take a bit of notice, but Hymie Levene? I think maybe you should try it first.

Hymie always was a bit soft in the head. I know him because we went to school together, and his family used to live opposite on Old Montague Street. He was in with the unions, and lost so many jobs. I says to him that if you just put half the work you put in for the union in working for yourself, you could open a bank.

With me it's all been different. I knew. So I stayed. You know what I paid for this place? Go on guess. In 1937 I paid £180. Just think of that – and you know what it's worth now? Well I don't know what it's worth now – because it's

187

going up more than a thousand a week and I haven't had it valued for three months – but three months ago it was worth ONE HUNDRED AND NINETY THOUSAND. And that's pounds, not francs or marks, or any other monopoly money. And I knew all them years ago.

Fifty years ago this very week, 1938, I remember it was summer, because there was Chamberlain back from Munich, I says to myself, Sammy, all you got to do is wait. How did I know? Because I use my eyes. I'm not like Hymie. Sammy's got a noddle, and Sammy knows how to use it.

I could see what the City was up to. The centre of the Empire as it was then. Hymie called it the centre of capitalism – and of course it is. But Hymie wanted to get rid of it and take their money. And I suppose I did too, but not in the same way.

I could see the City's got nowhere to go. Even in 1938 they were getting crowded. They can't go south because of the river. The docks were there in those days, but even with those gone you can't put the Bank of England on a barge. They can't go west because the West End won't move. They're doing too well in Selfridges, and C & A. They might have moved around the British Museum – but there's too many intellectuals and solicitors around there. The only place they can come is east. The working class – they can move them out of their Council flats, knock down their slums and clear them all out like rats off a bomb site. So all I had to do was wait.

I must admit I got a bit fed up in the fifties when nothing was happening. We were here in Spitalfields but they just weren't looking. In the 60s I begin to wonder whether it's me that's the fool. All the Jews are going, I'm finding it hard to do a bit of tailoring local. I have to go down to Dalston. But then in the 70s I know I got it right. All the Bangladeshis come, and I see some of the big houses, the old weaver's houses of the Huguenots – I know my history – they're getting done up and I'm thinking it won't be long now. Just hang on.

The other day the girl from Jewish Welfare comes along to see me. She dresses just like a *shiksa*. They all dress like street girls, even Jewish girls from good families. She comes from Finchley, and her mum and dad they used to live just in Valance Road. She tidies up, and I have to watch her. I don't want her rummaging around my papers. Some of them are valuable. A 1936 Jewish Chronicle is worth a lot to a collector, and the Yiddish papers there's interest in them too.

She says I don't have to live in this mess. She can't see some of it is worth a lot and appreciating all the time. You've got to know how to wait. Her name is Miriam and I like to have her come. I make her a cup of tea and give her a few biscuits. I don't begrudge it. After all she gives me a good laugh. And I must admit it's nice to look at a young face.

She says why don't I sell the place and have a bit of money? It's such a stupid thing to say, I choke and cough all my digestive biscuit over her. I tell her these houses are going up twenty five per cent each year. She says what good is that to me? I look at her. Can this be a Jewish girl saying this to me? I work it out for her. Twenty five per cent of ONE HUNDRED AND NINETY THOUSAND. Forgetting the shillings and pence it's – FORTY SEVEN AND A HALF THOUSAND. And she wants me to sell?

I can't understand her. She looks so like Hymie when she says it's paper money. I think any minute she'll be talking about happiness – and what bank will I take that to?

I tell her my dream. Here I am, 77 and so close. I want to be a quarter of a millionaire. What will Hymie say to that eh? Hymie in a rented house on a state pension. What will he say when Sammy Cohen is a quarter of a millionaire?

I tell you. He'll be *shtum*. Because I was the one who waited. I was the one who knew.

Soon I'll know a lot more. I got a valuer coming. And I've been told he's a crook.

A good, crooked capitalist. Just the thing when you want to sell a house. A shark – not a minnow. Sharks eat the minnows. And so long as it's your shark, he'll make money for you while he's making money for himself. You don't want a nice fella. That's fine to marry your daughter – but not for selling a house in 1988.

*

Soon as he comes in I'm impressed by his briefcase. I knew then I couldn't trust him. The combination lock on either side and the sharp click like a flick knife when it opened. Inside it he had a phone and a computer. More like a double agent than an estate agent. His suit was a good cloth, and he picked it up at the knees when he sat down. And all the time he told me not to worry: it's a seller's market.

He had a thin little moustache. How can you trust a man who spends two hours in front of the mirror playing with a couple of hairs? But it was his eyes that made me think this guy's a shark. They were laughing, even when he was serious. They were saying I know what your game is, and I'm in it 'n all.

And he wasn't Jewish. Mind you, I'm not surprised. With men like Hymie, and girls like the Jewish Welfare Board are sending, you can tell Jews have gone off money. It's the *goys* who are into money. Is it any wonder with Mrs Thatcher? Her I admire. She knows about making money, a grocer's daughter. All her youth the ring of the till. But my race they've grown ashamed of it.

This young man walks about my house, talking so fast, he gazumps himself. Now he's telling me about Docklands, and Wapping like it's news. To me! Who knew it in 1938. I should be pleased he's caught up.

Just to try him out, I says maybe I should do it up. He says don't bother. No one cares about the building. It could be a desirable heap of rubble providing it's in the right place.

Then he makes me a proposition. And I love him like a son. He says we could cut out the estate agent. He would sell the place for me. Not even put it on the market. He could get a better price – and then we split the difference.

190

Course he doesn't know that I don't want to sell until I've made my quarter of a million. I just got him here to do a free valuation. But I play him along. I say how much can you get for it.

And the next minute I'm shivering.

Two hundred and forty thousand!

I'm caught. Speechless. I have to sit down. I'm gasping with palpitations. He gets me a drink of water. I cannot believe how close I am. Sammy Cohen's nearly a quarter-millionaire. *Oi Vay*!

In the last three months my house has gone up fifty thousand. Think of that Hymie Levene! I can see the money, neatly stacked, lying there in clean bundles each tied with an elastic band.

He's looking at me, his face showing concern, but his eyes laughing. This shark is so clever, I wonder is he too clever?

My throat is hurting and I start speaking but he can't hear me. I say it again in a croaky voice, that hasn't drunk water in a year:

"I couldn't sell for less than quarter of a million."

The young man purses his lips, then taps away on his computer. Then pulls an ear, as if that is the final operation, and nods.

"Done." He puts out his hand. I take it. What a squeeze! I feel sorry for the minnows.

When he's gone I sit down and I'm overcome. I cry, big sobbing tears. When the girl from the Jewish Welfare comes I'm howling. I'm sitting on the sofa and I am shaking with tears. I am so overcome – I don't know whether I am the most happy man alive, or maybe I am experiencing the unhappiness of the rich. What a privilege! I cry some more. These are no ordinary tears. Each one is worth a shilling.

Miriam is feeling my head and taking my pulse. And asking me questions but I can't tell her anything, so she starts to undress me. No modesty about these girls.

And she gets me down to my underwear and I can see her turning her nose up but I am howling so hard with my miserable happiness. Can't she see it is no longer dirt, but eccentricity? She takes me up to bed and strips the sheet off, and she asks me where's the clean sheets? At a time like this, what should I tell her? Marks and Spencer's? But I can't say anything and she tries the drawers, and soon gets the idea, and puts the sheet back on again. You see, more eccentricity. More grist for the gossip columns.

She tucks me in, talking and telling me off – and I'm thinking this is no time to sleep. Me a quarter of a millionaire and I haven't told anyone. I want to write to Hymie. I try to get out of bed and she pushes me back. I got to tell him! I'm shouting and screaming that I got to tell Hymie Levene! And I say things about her. I would rather have a *shiksa* social worker. No good Jewish girl would wear a dress like that. She should show respect, didn't I know in 1938…!

The last I see of her she's holding me in the bed like a caterpillar wrapped in a leaf, with a determined look on her like a hungry thrush…

Some time later Margaret Thatcher is giving me a chopped herring sandwich and the Chancellor of the Exchequer hands me a wooden cotton reel to make a tank. Dad is singing to the treadle of his sewing machine. A bom-bom-bom, with his head down, working the material through. And I am climbing in and out of his cutting-table searching for pieces of chalk, scraps of material and pins to give to the Prime Minister in exchange for a peerage.

But it's a cheat of a dream. All the pins have gone, and I can't move to get to the chalk, and Margaret Thatcher has to go and see Hymie. I am awake enough to know it's phony. Lord Hymie of Harlow? Don't make me laugh.

So now I am lying in bed in the dark of the room. No Prime Minister or my dad on the treadle. The lights from the street throw long shadows across the room. Outside I can hear the call of Bengali voices, and footsteps passing beneath my window. I know I am awake and I feel the relief.

Thank God I never wrote to Hymie that I was going to sell. *Oi Vay* – what was I thinking! In two years I'll be half a millionaire, and in five I'll be a millionaire. So why am I suddenly rushing? All I got to do is wait. In 1993 I'll only be eighty-two.

And what a catch!

Manor Park Cemetery is in north-east Newham. I used to enjoy the wild areas, the bluebells, woods and brambles, but over the decades it has been manicured, and the gravestones increasingly regimented.

GRAVESTONES
Manor Park Cemetery

October breeze, fallen leaves crackle by new
    memorials:
beloved, sadly missed, dear husband, darling wife,
omitting anger, nagging, gambling, drinking, beating,
affairs, incest, instead dripping with platitude,
together at last,
once the soil is over their head,
once the coffin lid is nailed down tight,
and they cannot escape, then, only then –
they are always in our hearts.

Behind, older graves, from the 20s to the War.
With dusty plastic flowers, or fabric petals, colour
    long gone,
grass and herb robert in the footings,
dandelion and yellow vetch.
Forgotten ones who loved and suffered, betrayed,
bullied, drank, became ill and struggled, whose
    bodies
sagged under the burden,
hearts or cancers blowing them up until
they lay still, dead still, and the old bastard,
the dreadful cow, metamorphosed
into a vision of love chosen by God,
always in our hearts.

194

Horse chestnut leaves, crinkling brown,
never to be missed with angels at their head,
but swept into heaps, torched to cinders, life smoked
  away,
till no ghost or glimmer, but the chance of greedy
  atoms.

I was a stage manager for a few years. It is an obsessive, enclosed existence. Intense, almost to the point of madness, as we hope the audience will suspend its disbelief and validate us. This story was written in 1995.

Radio Play

I **VY** wakes me, she insists I must go to work. I groan and hide my head in the sheets. She pulls it off. I see her above me, holding a glass of fruit juice. I might be touched by her concern, if I could be touched by any emotion – but I am all pain.

"You must go in, Joe."

She has brought in a warm towel for my forehead. I place it over my face, and shiver with the sensation.

"You've already had a warning."

A little later she comes in with a coffee. The towel is already cold. I take it off and try a few sips of coffee. And feel sick.

"Phone in for me, please," I plead.

"No."

She's standing, hands on her hips, eyes screwed up. She's going to get me out of the house, one way or another.

"You'll feel better in the fresh air."

I have no resistance as Ivy heaves and shoves me; in and out of the bathroom, into clothes, and, at last, out of the house. On the path I hesitate and look back to her. Appealing. There's a chilly wind and the sky is grey and sombre. And she points forwards like the ghost of Christmas-yet-to-come.

I put one foot in front of the other. Surprisingly I move. Path and pavement pass under my feet, and coffee stays down.

What a night!

It was a late rehearsal for the next show. We went out for a meal, then back to a flat – I'm not sure whose. I remember tequila and lemon slices, I remember a furious argument about dog shit in the parks… I don't know how I got home.

I make it to the Frog and Princess. An old pub that used to have six bars but in the 70s they were all knocked into one enormous bar. It still has the claw-footed pillars and the Victorian frosted glass. Screw your eyes up and you can imagine Marie Lloyd singing Any Old Iron. Open them wide and you can see the gas lamps are fake.

As I come through the bar I wave to Ernie, the landlord, a little man with a bald head and loud voice. I don't know how much he drinks but he always has a pint on the bar, from one in the afternoon to eleven at night. And I'm sure it's not the same one.

He yells, "They're looking everywhere for you."

I say, "If you find me – please let me know."

I take the stairs two at a time which is just the right speed to set my head banging again. I glance at my watch. Fifteen minutes to curtain up. Hell. I go through the swing doors and yell out my apologies. George, the director, scowls at me, and so does Annie, his wife, whose latest moan is that I don't have enough receipts for my expenses. They're at the back straightening the chairs. I avoid that direction and go straight to the set.

I begin putting the props about. I know where they all go. For a stage manager this one is a doddle of a play. The set is a seedy hotel room. Some of the furniture we had ourselves, and I rented an old bed and a cupboard for a fiver from the furniture shop up the road. The back of the set is flats we had in store. I wallpapered them and then improved the colour by chucking tea and coffee over it. The play's a two-hander: once it gets started I've hardly anything to do. Lights up in the beginning, a couple of soft fades in the middle and lights down at the end.

I stand back. Everything looks OK. Table – yup. The book is on the bed. Crockery and saucepan on the cupboard. And the can of beer on the chair. The can is vital. Heineken! The play is set in Lagos, but could be anywhere. These two fellas with hardly two pennies to rub together are drinking their last can of beer when the Heineken man knocks at the door. If you have a can of Heineken when the man comes you get a prize. So they win a radio – but then fight over the radio. The play is funny but frankly I don't think George directed it that well. I made some suggestions. For instance; the Heineken man with the radio could have been a real snappy dresser – but then who takes any notice of stage managers?

The audience is coming in, so I go in my cubby hole. It's a recess off the main room. We've put a screen round it, so I can't be seen at the table with the light console but I can see the stage. I check the lights and make myself comfortable. Still a minute to curtain up, and I am all set. No panic. But that won't stop George and Annie telling me off after the show. They enjoy pulling rank.

But where would they be without me? George doesn't know which end to hold a screwdriver. I change all his light designs. He can't tell the difference. And as for that business about receipts – don't they trust me? All the hours I put in. Ah well… The walk did me good. My head's not so bad, that is if I don't move it. I'm dry as a leather belt but I'll have to wait now.

George comes in my door at the back. He's a thin, bearded man with one hell of a temper. All he talks about is theatre.

"One minute."

I nod and count off the time on my wrist watch. Then I take the house lights down. In the five seconds of darkness the two actors creep in. I slide the stage lights up and there they are as if they have always been there.

I don't listen to the play. I know the cues well enough. I stretch out and massage my forehead. And then after a few minutes I lay my head on the table. I have ages to the first cue. There's no danger of me falling asleep and I can hear the dialogue clear enough.

George comes quietly in.

"Where's the radio?"

I say, "In the dressing room."

He shakes his head.

"Must be," I insist.

"It isn't there," he says coldly.

I try to think where it could be. There just aren't many places for it.

"How many times have I told you," says George, "to go through your checklist?"

Where the heck is it? The Heineken man is supposed to come in ten minutes with the radio.

"Well?" hisses George.

"If it's not in the dressing room," I muse, "and not here…" I look around me to check, and it isn't. But then – it comes to me where it is. I slap my palm to my head in agony.

"Oh no!"

"Shut up!" George pushes me, indicating the audience.

"I know where it is," I say quietly.

"Then go and get it," he says sharply, "and take it to the dressing room."

"I can't."

"Why the hell not!"

"Yesterday after the show," I say, wondering how to phrase it, "well… I put it in the cupboard." I stop again, but it has to be said. "The one on the stage."

George snatches at the air. "Oh fuck!"

My mind is in overdrive. How can we get the radio out of the cupboard? It's a one-act play with no blackouts. Anyone who tries to get it would be seen. The radio would be seen. It would make the play senseless. The Heineken man has to bring it.

"You've got to get another radio," says George.

"Right," I say, getting up.

"And don't come back without one."

I go down to the bar. I explain to Ernie that I need a radio urgently.

"We have got a radio," he says. "Just the thing for you."

200

I sigh with relief. "I'll love you forever, Ernie."

"Just don't tell the wife," he says, and pops out back.

I'm crossing my fingers and hoping. To be precise it isn't a radio we use in the play but a tape recorder so that we get the right music, but the difference is too difficult to explain.

Ernie comes back with a Walkman and headphones, and my heart sinks.

"It's no good," I tell him.

His face drops like a child's. I can't handle his disappointment. Not with six minutes to go. So I take the Walkman. It's useless, the radio has to be heard. They dance to it. But I haven't time for explanations.

I thank him for his help and leave the pub. I run along to the furniture shop up the road. The old lady is sitting on a chair amidst the old furniture eating a sandwich.

"Have you got a radio?" I say. "A portable."

She rubs a hairy chin. "Have we? Have we?" She looks about her. "We did have, you know. Come back in an hour and I'll sort it out for you."

My throat goes dry. "I must have it now."

"Can't you wait a bit?"

"It's an emergency," I say.

She looks at me strangely. "An emergency? For a portable radio?"

"Believe me," I say forlornly.

She sighs and gets out of her chair, her old bones reluctant. She goes into a back room. While she is out I search the shop. Under tables, in cupboards. If it is in one why not in another?

Four minutes to the Heineken man.

She comes in with a radio.

"Found it. Four quid."

I give her the money and take it from her. I turn it on. Nothing.

"You'll have to get batteries," she says.

I waste a minute taking the back off the radio. The Asian shopkeeper tells me the batteries I want and gives them to me. I give him a fiver, tell him to keep the change and rush out of the shop.

On my way back to the pub I put the batteries in the radio. I click the back on and turn on the set. Not a crackle. I open it up again and turn the batteries round. Not a dickey-bird.

I want to cry. I want my mummy, my teacher and my teddy bear.

I push all the buttons, I twist the tuning dial and it comes off in my hand.

Despair courses through me. I feel tiny and humiliated. The play is going to be a fiasco and it is all going to be my fault. I dash the radio to the ground, the batteries pop out and I kick them savagely into the road. I wish I had stayed in bed.

It is then the obvious hits me, and I sprint.

I should have got run over twice but I bear a charmed life. I push people aside, I don't give a sod, and just go, oblivious of the annoyance of old ladies. I have a life to save.

My own.

I come down the footbridge gasping for breath, down the pavement and swing into the garden path. I have my keys already in my hand and have the door open in an instant. In two strides I'm in the sitting room.

And there is Ivy and a man I can't recognise from behind, both naked and flat out on the carpet.

Ivy sits up covering her breasts and gasps, "Aren't you at the theatre?"

"I will be," I say and grab the radio from the sideboard.

It isn't until I am out the house and running back up the footbridge that I realise that I don't know who she was with.

My headache has come back, my heart is threatening to burst out of my chest as I pound in through the pub. George is waiting at the top of the stairs. I do a last sprint and hand out the radio.

"You're too late," he says. "They mimed it."

I put down the radio and collapse on the top step.

"It worked brilliantly," he says. He turns away. "Don't forget your last cue."

I go back in. The audience is laughing. The two actors are dancing to imaginary music. It's so funny even I laugh. They've got a pretend-ghettoblaster and they're pounding out the beat on the furniture. I can almost hear it, it's so painfully funny. I am so impressed by the way they have taken up my cock-up and used it. The play ends. I fade down the lights, and quickly bring them up for the applause. I am clapping with the rest, clapping so hard I nearly forget to bring the house lights up.

The audience leave in a buzz of conversation. I go on set and take the radio out of the cupboard. I put it with my checklist next to the lightboard for tomorrow. I hesitate, wondering whether it would be wise to go and see the cast who have gone down to the bar for a drink. Shame holds me back. But I cast it aside; now's the time – while they are on a high.

I grab my own radio; the vision at home floods back. Who was she with on the carpet? I can't bear to think about it. I dash down to the bar, wanting to surround myself with people. As I step in, radio in my arms, I get instant applause.

"Drinks? Drinks?" I exclaim to the circle of theatricals. I put down the radio and rush away at their nods, before they can hector me.

As Ernie is pulling the Guinnesses, I count my cash. I have just enough. I'll give them their drinks, there'll be a couple of minutes joshing – then it'll all be over.

Ernie draws a shamrock on the froth as he finishes each pint. He puts the glasses, one by one, on a round tray.

"You were in rather a rush before," he says as I hand over my cash.

I admit I was.

"That radio I lent you… You wouldn't have it?"

"Just let me take these over," I say lifting the tray of clinking drinks and heading for the cast.

Now where the heck did I leave it?

Life can deliver some low blows. What, then, can give us hope to carry on? A glimpse of beauty perhaps.

The Singer

IN the yellow of the street lamp, the rain showed like scratches on film. George tied his bike, water glistening on his hands as he fumbled with lock and chain. He was tempted to leave it unlocked, with a safety warning for the thief.

He took his clips off slowly, teasing out the seconds. Rain dripped off his chin into his chest. He put the clips in his pocket and smoothed his hair. A painful numbness was tunnelling from the inside to meet the outside cold. Pulling his thin jacket round him, he looked across at the house. A terraced house set straight on the pavement.

Bike chained, clips off, rain streaming, he was unable to move. What would she say to him? Would she slam the door in his face? Could he blame her if she did?

Why go through with it?

A bolt of lightning startled the street, followed almost at once by thunder. He must. Head down, he began to walk across the road. A million droplets like multitudes of soldiers splattered out their brains on the tarmac.

No bell. She had never wanted one. George rapped on the door pane. The first time so soft he could barely hear it, the second time, breath held, sharper. He stepped back a foot and turned sideways, so as not to look so helpless. A drainpipe gurgled and flooded across the pavement.

Movement in the house. He stiffened, like a child about to have a plaster torn off, and wiped the water across his eyebrows. When he took his hands away, she was standing before him.

In bare feet and a red frock. She had cut her hair.

"Passing," he stuttered.

"You'd better come in," she said.

He tripped over the door-ledge as he followed her along the hallway. The curve of her hips, her neck and freckled back in the dip of her dress were at once beautiful and overpowering. Her scent floated back. He felt weak and infantile.

He had no time to prepare himself before he was in the sitting room. Rob was seated at the table, the remnants of a meal covering it, and two bottles of wine. Face red with warmth and wine, he was wearing a white shirt, sleeves rolled up and open at the neck, revealing thick curling hair.

"Have a glass," said Rob holding up a bottle.

George wanted to walk out but took a glass. Rob filled it, his angular face confident in ownership. All further questions – irrelevant.

She was seated again at the table, he sat on the arm of an armchair, holding the wine glass two thirds full of deep red wine. His knee was trembling unbearably.

"How have you been?" she said.

"All right."

She saw him looking about the room and said, "I painted it." He nodded to show he was listening. "I got fed up with the brown."

Nothing in the room was his anymore. Rob had his feet on a chair and was picking bits of fruit salad with his fingers.

"Would you like some?" he said, teeth coloured with red wine.

George shook his head. "I've eaten."

The room was foreign to him. Apart from the different colour, the furniture was mostly new. The photo he had given her of children playing with hoops and skipping ropes, which had been on the wall over the sofa; the space was now occupied by an old London Transport poster of women in large hats and gentlemen with canes. The sofa had become a sideboard. The gas fire had been replaced by central heating. Had Rob moved in? He supposed so.

He had to leave.

"Are you working, George?" she said.

"Yes," he lied.

He waited for her to ask "at what?". But instead she took a stick of celery and began to crunch it between sips of wine.

"And you?" he asked.

She smiled wryly, her teeth stringy with celery. "I'm at the same school as Rob now. Deputy head of department."

Rob was holding up one of the bottles of wine and reading it intensely, screwing up his face as if he were about to give it a bad mark.

"God knows what they chuck in these Rhine wines."

George stretched forward and made for the table with his glass. It tottered on the edge. He caught the glass but the wine was on the carpet.

"Sorry," he stuttered, rising. "I only popped in to see how you were."

"And to spill our wine," said Rob with a laugh.

She touched his arm. "Leave it."

For a second he was unable to speak, thrown by the touch and the intensity of her eyes. He could see the concern. Aah, she felt sorry for him.

At last he said in a trembling voice, "I must go. I've someone to see."

"It's pouring," she said.

Rob had taken up the other wine bottle, and was shaking his head as he went over the label. *See me.*

'Stay for a coffee," she said.

Does she still dip digestive biscuits in her coffee? She had got him into the habit; the two of them on the carpet in front of the gas fire, that was no more.

He backed out. She came with him to the door picking up an umbrella in the hallway.

"Please take it," she said at the front door.

"I'm on my bike."

He wanted to stay. He couldn't bear to stay. She kissed him on the cheek. A spark of warmth for a frostbitten man.

"Take it easy. The roads are dangerous."

Swinging onto the saddle he gave her a wave.

She waved back. "Come again, George – and stay a bit longer."

Cycling away, he didn't look behind, pulling round the first corner.

It rained steadily and gusted as he rambled along the streets. Turning this way, that; down shopping streets of bright windows, and quiet side streets, of houses possessed by flickering lights.

He cut through a council estate where children were playing, splashing each other in dirty puddles and screaming in fun and mock shock, while he clung hard to the handlebars.

The rain was an icy balm. He could weep unseen, tears mingling with the stream running off his face.

On the hill he let go. Not for the excitement, but for the hell of it. There was the considerable chance he might come a cropper and he would thank God for it. The wind was with him, the rain drove behind. The front wheel ripped through the surface water like a saw.

Yellow lights shone on the other side of the road, vehicles groaning in their gears like hogs forced home. If he turned his wheel just an inch, a little inch, he would smash straight into one – and be an inch, a littler inch in tomorrow's paper.

At the bottom of the hill ahead of him was a zebra crossing. Someone in red stepped out. He knew he couldn't stop, not at this speed, with his brakes. Without bothering to touch them, he pulled wide and around, causing the person to cry out, and give herself away as an old woman. Fortunately, or otherwise, the other side of the road was clear.

He still had the speed of the hill, when a little further along the police car swung in front. A head poked out of the window and shouted for him to pull up.

He stopped when he could, using his feet on the roadway.

The car door banged and the policeman ran up to him gesticulating.

"You nearly killed that old lady."

He was wearing a flat hat, face shiny and smelling of aftershave.

"You don't call these brakes?"

The policeman was down on his knees looking at the back brake, forcing George to look. Only one block was making any contact, and not much at that.

"How can you ride a bike like this? You're not a kid."

Hands on hips, the policeman was shaking his young head at the stupidity of the world.

"That front light..." he began and lost himself in the pointlessness of it. "Walk. Do you hear me? Walk. If I see you riding, I'll run you in."

The policeman, sighing heavily, returned to his car. The car waited. George began to walk the bike on the pavement.

A half moon came out of a horse head of cloud. And was instantly dragged back in, as if dirty work were afoot in the heavens.

He shook his head and the rain flew out as if from a washed lettuce. He was chilly with walking and thought of getting back on the bike, and glanced behind. The figure in red came to him, and the cry as he pulled round. The policeman was right; the bike was a menace. He had meant to fix it. Meant to do so many things.

Passing a pub, someone came out and warm boozy air blew at him. On impulse he decided to go in. He leaned his bike against a wall without bothering to chain it. If it were taken – so be it – one less responsibility.

It was a drab public bar. A check linoleum floor in black and a grey that might have been white beneath the scuffing. Plain wooden tables were around the outside with wooden chairs, and in the centre chequered emptiness. At the bar an elderly woman polished glasses.

There were four customers apart from himself. Two black men playing dominoes, slapping them down and laughing in a manner so public, so unEnglish – it was like talking in church. An old man slumped in a corner chair, breathing so heavily he could be heard across the bar. At his feet was an ancient black dog sleeping, its sides heaving as if in rhythm with its master.

The fourth customer had come in just after himself. A short man in a long black coat, more like a dressing gown. He wore a green alpine hat, somewhat crumpled, that had been popular thirty years before. His face was gaunt with perhaps four days' growth of beard and his eyes encircled in wire glasses. He was talking to the domino players.

George sat down with his drink, selecting a table equidistant from the occupied ones. Cycling and walking had frozen his thoughts. Now the thaw.

"*Come again, George – and stay a bit longer.*" A sob slipped out. He wiped an eye and glanced about. No one had seen.

It was over. Why prolong it? He had had his chances and muffed them. She was out of his life and it was his fault. She was too clever, he was too critical. Surprising it had lasted as long as it did.

There couldn't be another night like the last. At three in the morning he had gone to the bathroom for the tablets, had filled his hand – and thrown them into the toilet. At four he had regretted it. At five as the sun came up he had resolved to see her.

The man in the long black coat was standing over him. In a thick Irish accent he said, "Have you got a quid for a drink?" And held out a grimy hand, nails bitten down to the quick.

The man's eyes were dark and shifty. He had taken his hat off, his hair was short with bare patches at the side, obviously a home-made job. His remaining teeth were stumps, like stones in an old graveyard.

On the cadge. That was why he had been talking to the black men. A year ago, George would probably have said yes, but not now.

He shook his head, saying not a word, and the man, as if expecting it, moved on.

How low, he thought. In cast off clothing, begging. He would jump off a bridge first. He clenched his nails into his palms. Never beg. Die first.

There was a rapid slap of dominoes, followed by raucous laughter. One black man slapped the other on the back. "Your round, man. "

Someone was singing. A strong, lyrical voice. It was the Irishman. He was standing by the bar clutching his hat, and singing to some point above their heads.

Instantly struck, George could not check his tears even if he had wished to. How much the man felt, how much pain he had endured. The long slow notes of the Irishman's tenor carried it all. A sadness too much to bear.

It was a song of old Ireland, a mournful song of a country home, a lost love, and a mother waiting. It filled the bar. The two black men stopped their dominoes. The old man slumped in the corner opened his eyes, and the dog lifted its head from the mat. Only the woman at the bar continued polishing glasses.

The song streamed into George's secret places; his cast-out childhood, his adult pain, loves that had come and loves that had gone, loves that would never be. The sadness of the song seemed to hollow him as if his head was a vast hallway filled with liquid melancholy. Not Irish, not English, but of every place, every time.

He could not go on like this. He would not go on like this.

He shut his eyes and the music enclosed him; impossible heartache, sorrow beyond endurance. Waves and waves of it, flowed through him and around him. And carried him far beyond himself.

The singer stopped. He stood motionless looking into the distance. Looking perhaps into memories older even than his hat. A shudder, then a shake of the head seemed to bring him back.

George sat motionless as if the song were still being sung. Within him was the sadness, the beauty, and the astonishment that he could be so affected.

The dominoes had begun again as George went to the bar. The Irishman was standing over them watching them slap down the pieces. The old man was snoring again, his dog nodding at his feet.

George bought a pint and left it on the counter.

"For you," he called as he crossed to the door.

The Irishman licked his lips and gave him the thumbs up.

"Good on ya, mate!"

George stepped out into the night. The rain had stopped and the half moon was out amongst rocky clouds. He pulled his damp jacket around him, lifting the collar. For a few seconds he gazed at the bike which had fallen in a heap on the pavement, shook his head, and walked quickly home.

These stories were about to be published in the year 2000 but the publisher went bankrupt. Just before the axe came down, they asked me to write a piece for their revamped website. The website never appeared, but here's the piece; a story in a story that takes us back to the beginning.

The Shoot

10.00 am

I am at Liverpool Street station and my head is banging like a kettle drum. Last night, when Max turned up with his 100 per cent proof tequila, I should have been more assertive. Instead I got out the salt and lemon. Now I am a walking zombie. This is not my part of town. I do fashion shoots mostly. I don't understand why I am taking pictures of Brick Lane. But I am in no condition to argue. Not with Audrey.

How do you get out of this station?

10.20

I get as far as the Barbican when I realise this is probably the wrong way. I go up to a paper-stand, feeling like a tourist.

"Which way to the East End?"

I am sold an A to Z. (I must have ten of them at home).

10.30

Back at Liverpool Street Station I have a coffee. I don't feel a lot better. I should have stayed in bed. I couldn't have stayed in bed. Heavy drinking does not help me sleep. I open the A to Z. Let's plan this damn shoot. What's in the notes?

What a folder Audrey's given me!

Here we go. First page. I have to take some pictures to go with a story by Derek Smith. Who? *Strikers of Hanbury Street.*

Am I supposed to have read it? It's only damn well here. Pages of it. I don't read stories. I take pictures. It's all about Jews. Alright, I'll find some Jews.

So pictures of Brick Lane she wants: Hanbury Street, Princelet Street, Gardiner's Corner and Whitechapel. Right, let's get on the move.

10.40

I go down Middlesex Street. I've heard of that. Petticoat Lane. Then down Artillery Passage. Just the sort of place you could imagine Jack the Ripper hanging round. Then out on to Spitalfields Market. I thought it was fruit and veg but it's all trendy shops. And then, there in front of me is this big white church with a tall spire. I have the feeling I should recognise it.

Christ Church of Spitalfields, it says on the board. Built between 1711 and 1729 by Hawksmoor. Well what do you know? I'll get a couple of pictures for the album.

To make a donation... No thanks, I am the one getting paid today.

10.50

I go down Fournier Street, some posh houses here. Big green doors with Dickensian doorknobs. Then I'm on Brick Lane. Now what? A few Asian guys wandering round, wearing white cotton hats. I see up ahead a sign for Princelet Street. So let's take some photos.

But Princelet Street goes both ways. Either side of Brick Lane. Which one do they want? Not that there's much to see. Metal posts on the pavement. All the houses shuttered. Quite a bit of building work going on. Money's moving in. I wonder who is moving out?

I take a few pictures. They're nothing. What am I supposed to be getting?

All this walking is not helping my head.

Izzy's family – there were seven and they just lived in one room in Princelet Street. It was right at the top of the house and used to stink of piss and cooking. The whole house just had one outside toilet. But it was not only people in Izzy's place; his mum had her sewing machine which was always rattling away and there were piles of clothing she'd be working on, amongst everything else. It was a madhouse.

Izzy had a job which he used to do before school. He had a wheelbarrow and had to take papers from Yankel's, the Yiddish printers, to the newsagents. I've seen his barrow piled so high he could hardly move it. And they used to yell at him for being late. Well everyone did. The Yiddish printers, the newsagents, and then our teacher. And what was worse out of all this he hardly saw a penny. His dad took it and gambled it. His mother used to keep the house, when she wasn't machining, and his dad took most of her money as well. I have seen Izzy, his feet coming out of his shoes with snow on the ground. My dad saw him. He said, "Come in, Izzy." Then he repaired his shoes. He said, "Never walk round like that again. You come and see me."

I get out my A to Z. Hanbury Street is just down the road. I pass Mahib Indian Cuisine. Black windows like an ambulance. Open 12 – 3 pm. I doubt they're up yet. Sensible people.

Hanbury Street runs east and west too. This is dumb. Which one, which way? There's nothing on the west side except Salique's Bangladeshi restaurant and more builders. Oh man, there is a smell of curry I would kill for!

Truman's Brewery on the corner of Hanbury Street and Brick Lane. Too early, even for me. What's supposed to be happening in this story on Hanbury Street? I can't read it now. Let's have a skim… Jewish kids, playing football.

I walk east on Hanbury Street. Nazrul Balti House, Spice Garden restaurant, Eastern film club. I'm looking for a cobbler's… but there's no cobbler's. Bangla Town Cash and Carry, full of sacks of rice, and drums of vegetable oil. Then it's council flats and more council flats.

We cut through the back streets to Hanbury Street where I lived.
My dad would be wondering about the leather.

I left the two of them outside while I went in the house. Dad had the
front room of the house as his workshop. He was there in the dust, the
sunlight spinning through on to his bench. Always that smell of leather
dust. A shoe on a last and pins in his mouth. He could bang them in
so fast you could hardly see his hand moving. On one side of him his
row of knives, on the other his leather needles. Behind him on shelves,
shoes that he had mended. At his feet a pile of shoes waiting to be done.
And the floor a mess of leather strips and cut outs.

11.05

Two Asian kids are playing with Pokemon cards. I ask
them if there's any synagogues round here. They don't know.
I offer them a couple of quid to play football in the street.
They turn me down. I offer them a fiver. They say it's too
dangerous. Can you believe it? I would have sold my granny
for that. I up it to 8 quid and they take it. I get my pictures
and almost get run over.

My mum was right of course; Hanbury Street is not a main road
but busy enough. We dodged between the wheelbarrows and the horse
and carts risking life and limb.

But it was such a ball. None of us had played with a real football
before. If we wanted a game we would make up a bundle of rags and
kick that about – but a leather football. Who could believe it?

Each time I caught it I would feel it, like a pet animal. Mine, my
beautiful ball. That is until Izzy threw it into the horse manure.

I go back down Hanbury Street to Brick Lane. Then I
walk up Brick Lane towards Aldgate. There's not going to be
any Jews around. There's a mosque, there's food shops with
all that sweet stuff in it, there's restaurants, there's sari and
fabric shops… There's not a sign of anything Jewish. I know
this place used to be Jewish. Didn't they fight Mosley and his
fascists round here?

216

We turned into the bustle of Brick Lane. People, shops with their wares taking over half the pavement, a smell of pickles and straw, of horse manure and dust. In the road were men with carts, pushing them, pulling them. A few newish ones and a lot more that just seemed to be held together with spit. Horses and carts rattled by, and the occasional impatient lorry.

They shouted all around us. Horse whips cracked about our ears. Men with barrows cursed us as they pulled by. On the pavements passers-by stared at us. Some blankly, others hollered for us to get out of the road. The two of us walked on trying to look only ahead, assured of the rightness of our cause, and feeling very misunderstood.

11.30

I am on the Whitechapel High Road, top of Brick Lane. I've been flicking through the story and it's historical. That makes more sense. Somewhere round here is Gardiner's Corner according to it. Sounds like a plant nursery – but must be a shop or a pub.

"Where we going to march from?" asked Izzy.

"From here. Up to Gardiner's Corner," I said. "All marches go there. Then back down Brick Lane."

So I walk around looking for it. Past Aldgate East Station, past the library, past the Whitechapel Art Gallery; so that's where it is. Getting educated today.

I cross over, taking my life in my hands with the traffic. I want danger money. It should be somewhere near this roundabout. That's Commercial Road, that's the Whitechapel Road... So where is Gardiner's flaming Corner supposed to be?

My head was getting better – but this traffic is doing it in again.

11.45

I go in the library by the Whitechapel Art Gallery.

"Excuse me, I'm looking for Gardiner's Corner," I say.

The young Muslim girl in a headscarf looks puzzled but her older colleague says, "You're 30 years too late."

"The story of my life."

"They knocked it down in the 70s."

"Typical."

"We've got the East London Advertiser on microfiche, if you want to look it up…"

"No thanks." I turn away and then think better of it. "This is Aldgate yes?"

"Yes."

"So where is Whitechapel?"

"Next to Old Kent Road," says the woman.

"There," I say, "is a sign of a misspent youth."

"Back on the main road," she says, "turn left for half a mile."

12.00

There's the Salvation Army; just opposite is the East London Mosque with a huge minaret and two towers with crescents on. Then I hit Whitechapel market. I like this, lots of people. Black, white, Asian. A mass of colour with all the Asian cloth and stalls. Cockney voices, West Indian, and Bangladeshi…

I take some shots. I include the London Hospital across the road… A helicopter is taking off from the roof. I snap it. Why not? Local colour.

Well, on this day we were watching the march. The London Jewish Bakers were on strike and they were marching down the Whitechapel Road towards Aldgate. There were hundreds of them, and they weren't wearing overalls and aprons, but just ordinary clothes. At the front they had a big banner saying who they were over a picture of men putting bread in an oven. Underneath it said "Buy Bread with the Union label."

218

I knew a bit about it because my dad told me. They worked all the hours, lots of night work – well you know, to get the bread out for the morning. Terrible conditions, bad pay – the usual. But it was skilled work. Jews like their bread. Cholas, rye bread, beigels, platzels, matzos, biscuits and cakes. Hooman taschen – that's what I liked; sticky pastry, full of sweet poppy seeds. Mmmm.

I wander up a bit. I see the Blind Beggar pub... Wasn't there some murder there by the Krays? Just opposite is Sydney Street. I seem to remember something happening there once. Anarchists, shooting. I've seen a picture of Winston Churchill in a top hat directing soldiers...

That's enough. I've taken two rolls of film.

I shall leave the East End to the East Enders, whoever they are.

I go down Whitechapel Tube. And head up west for the afternoon shoot. My headache has gone. That's what a stroll in the fresh air does for you.

On the tube, I've got nothing else, so I read *Strikers of Hanbury Street*.

And if you want the opinion of this illiterate sod – well, it's not bad.

Also by Derek Smith:
Catching Up

Welcome to the flying sale, the must go
of tourist fashion; a 1000 places
you surely must see before you die, or
you are no one. Who has yet to descend
the Grand Canyon? Walk the Inca trail
to Machu Picchu? Oh! Not spied the polar bears
on the ice floes? Quick! While there are ice floes,
while there are polar bears. Never ridden safari
in Ngorogoro Crater? - oh what
have you been doing with your time?

- from "Fly Past"

"Catching Up" is a collection of poems which
contemplate a range of concerns; time and space, the
hidden meanings in stories, meditations on war and the
legacy of our environmental sins.